ANATOMY OF A GIRL GANG

ARSENAL PULP PRESS VANCOUVER

ANATOMY
OF A
GIRL
GANG

A NOVEL

ASHLEY
LITTLE

ARSENAL PULP PRESS
Suite 202 – 211 East Georgia St.
Vancouver, BC V6A 1Z6
Canada
arsenalpulp.com

The publisher gratefully acknowledges the support of the Canada Council for the Arts and the British Columbia Arts Council for its publishing program, and the Government of Canada (through the Canada Book Fund) and the Government of British Columbia (through the Book Publishing Tax Credit Program) for its publishing activities.

This is a work of fiction. Any resemblance of characters to persons either living or deceased is purely coincidental.

Editing by Susan Safyan
Book design by Gerilee McBride

Printed and bound in Canada

Library and Archives Canada Cataloguing in Publication

Little, Ashley, 1983–
    Anatomy of a girl gang / Ashley Little.

Issued in print and electronic formats.
ISBN 978-1-55152-529-7 (pbk.).—ISBN 978-1-55152-530-3 (epub)

    I. Title.

PS8623.I898A73 2013   C813'.6   C2013-903249-5
                                           C2013-903250-9

For the children of the Downtown Eastside
and gang girls everywhere

The darkness of the mind & the darkness of death,
& in between the bright day, bright city

—George Stanley, *Vancouver: A Poem*

PROLOGUE

SLY GIRL

I was shot in the face three years ago. The guy on the news said it was gang-related. But it wasn't. Not really. It was just a bullet that went the wrong way. I left the rez in July thinking that I wouldn't have to deal with that kind of bullshit no more. And where do I end up? Vancouver, BC, Gang Capital of Canada.

Ha ha, right?

My gang is called the Black Roses, and we are this city's worst nightmare. There are five of us. Mac, she's our OG, says there can only ever be five—a handful—any more and it would get out of hand. Mac didn't even want me in the gang, eh. Not at first she didn't. Mercy had to convince her to let me in. Said they needed someone who knew her way around dope, and there I was, all gettin ready to be fourteen, already knowin everythin there is to know about everythin: crack, meth, heroin, coke, weed, whatevers.

How'd I learn?

Oh, man, everybody knows that stuff if they's born on the rez I'm from. Don't necessarily *want* to know it, but you do, you do. My five brothers, they liked to mess around with it all. Showed me a lot. Too much, maybe. But I don't really think too much on them no more.

My gang calls me Sly Girl. That wasn't always my name. But now, it always will be.

PART 1
YEAR OF THE GUN

Of course I didn't want her to do it. You don't let someone you care about—hell, someone you love—sell themselves on the corner like another dirty piece of kiff. Fuck that noise, man. I said we would never do that. Never. That's about when I realized the Vipers didn't really give a solid fuck about us. They weren't our *family*, they weren't our *friends*, they were just using us like everyone else.

They tried to get me to do it first. I flat out refused. Told Cyco to go down to Davie and get his own ass fucked. Mercy worked East Cordova for two nights. The second night she got home, the side of her face looked like a grated eggplant. Her lip was bleeding all over the place, it was nasty.

What the fuck happened to you?

It's nothing. I'm fine. She let her long black hair fall across her face as she dug around in the freezer for ice.

Fuck that. You are not fine. Who did this to you?

She shrugged.

Who did this!?!

I don't know. Some yuppie, drives a BMW.

You know what? Fuck this shit. This is over. This ends. Now.

She sighed. Mac, when I joined, I agreed to put in work for the gang. Whatever it takes, I said. This is the work they need done right now.

This is not work, Mercy. This is human slavery.

She winced as she pressed a bag of frozen peas to her cheek. She sat down at the table where I was weighing and bagging up weed.

Got a joint for me?

I'm serious, Merce. How much did you make tonight?

Four-fifty. She sat up a little straighter.

Yeah, and how much of that do you get to keep, personally?

She shrugged. None, I guess.

Doesn't really seem worth it, does it? I handed her the joint I'd rolled for her.

Well, Mac, you tell me then, what the fuck else am I going to do? Her dark eyes shone in the harsh light of the bare bulb. I'm a high school dropout and a Punjabi orphan from Surrey. This is the best gig going.

I looked around the dank little SRO we shared. It was a shitty box with brown water stains spreading across the ceiling and mould growing in the windows. We could hear our neighbours fight and fuck and fix. The whole building reeked of piss, and cockroaches scuttled around 24/7. The Vipers paid our rent and filled our fridge and "looked after us." But we had to work for it, nothing came easy. I had been thinking of leaving them for awhile. Things just weren't right. Mercy and I should've been treated like *queens*, you know? Now our boys were picking fights with other crews, and bodies were dropping all over the city. Civilians too. It was mad carnage. Now, because I was a Viper, I was a target. What the hell kind of protection is that? That's the opposite of protection. It's bullshit is what it is. Fuck it.

I watched my best friend blow smoke out the side of her mouth, her lower lip swollen like a rotten plum. A tear escaped from her left eye, which was nearly swollen shut, and she brushed it away like a fly. That's when I decided: I was exiting the Vipers and taking Mercy with me.

I packed up all our shit that night and called Cyco in the morning. He came over with another OG named Vex.

What's all this about, girls? Cyco put his feet up on our kitchen table and lit a cigarette. Vex stood by the door, hands in his pockets.

We want out, I said.

He snickered, and Vex cough-laughed into his hand.

I glared at Cyco while I lit a smoke.

He looked from me to Mercy. What? Because of that? He gestured to her face. That's nothing. That's a kiss! Eh, Mercy? You're fine, eh, chicky-poo? C'mere a minute. He patted his thigh as if she were a dog that would come and settle on his lap.

We're done, I said, and put my gat on the table in front of him. I remembered when he'd given it to me. The first week I joined, more than a year ago. My very own Glock .32. It was a beautiful machine. I'd fired it a handful of times. Not to kill anyone, just to scare em. Let em know they couldn't even dream about fuckin with me. I shot a guy in the hand once for snitching. He gave testimony in a trial that put one of our crew away for fifteen years. Blew his fuckin fingers off, man. I thought he got off easy.

Mercy slid her 9 from her waistband and laid it on the table.

So that's it, eh? After everything we've done for you? Just gonna take back what you promised us? Think you can make it all disappear? He snapped his fingers.

You haven't really held up your end of the bargain, *homes*.

He snorted. Well, good fuckin luck to ya if you think you have got a hope in hell of making it alone out there. You two are nothing without the Vipers backing you. You're nada. Fuck all. Less than zero. I'll be surprised if you last an hour out there on your own.

We'll be fine, I said, and glanced at Mercy as she crossed her arms over her chest, her nostrils flaring like they do when she's about to get mad. The diamond stud in her nose glittered in the sunlight that leaked across our kitchen. I stubbed out my cigarette in the tinfoil ashtray.

Phones. Cyco held out his hands and we placed our burners in each of his palms. And what's your uncle gonna have to say about all this, Miss Mac?

He'll say I should've left a long time ago, when you all started getting sloppy, killing people for no reason, shooting civilians, acting like pimps when you're supposed to be gangsters.

Jeez, girl. You got some big balls for a chick. C'mere.

What?

C'mere, I need to give you a goodbye kiss.

Huh? We'd kissed before, oh hell, we'd done more than that, we'd done everything. But it was a long time ago, and it only happened twice, maybe three times. We were drunk. No one in the Vipers knew about it. Except Mercy. I looked at Mercy; she'd pressed her lips together so hard they'd turned pale purple.

You know, if you were anyone else, you wouldn't be able to get away with this. Not without severe motherfucking consequences. Cyco's blue eyes flashed as he took off his ball cap. Now get your ass over here, girl. Show me some respect.

I got up and walked toward him, avoiding his eyes. When I got close enough, he grabbed my left hand and brought it to his lips, kissing me in the web between my thumb and first finger. Then he put the end of his cigarette on the place he'd kissed and held it there.

Fuck, C! I jerked my hand away, but he held it tight. The smell of my searing flesh flipped my stomach, and for a second I thought I'd puke all over him, but I looked into his eyes instead, and made my gaze stone-hard.

After about a thousand years, he let go of my hand. He looked from me to Mercy to Vex. He shrugged, and Vex nodded.

Well, what the fuck are you waiting for? Take your *shit* and *get the fuck out of here*, he yelled. Don't ever come back! Don't try to contact us, *any* of us—ever. Don't acknowledge us if we pass you on the street. You two are dead to us now. You're on your own, you dirty orphans. Now, *get out!*

Vex held the door open.

Mercy and I picked up our stuff—two suitcases and two backpacks between us. We walked out the door, holding our heads high.

That night, we crashed at a crack house that was open to anyone brave enough to go inside. It was so disgusting; you'd throw up if I told you about it. We had to sleep in shifts, one of us always awake, to make sure the crackies stayed off of us. I woke up near dawn to Mercy tugging at my hair.

Sorry. Just getting a roach out.

I rolled over and covered my ears to block out the sounds of people moaning, humping, tripping, fiending. I could smell the blood and shit-stained mattress through my sleeping bag, and promised myself I would never do this again.

The next day, I insisted that we splurge for a room at the Cambie. We had about a grand in savings between us. We spent fifty bucks for two beds with clean blankets, a desk, a lamp, a shared kitchen, a bathroom, and a laundry room. It was worth every penny. Everything smelled like bleach, and it was wonderful. I just needed some time to think. Make a plan.

MERCY

I thought Mac had finally gone insane when she told me she wanted to start a new gang. But I *knew* she had lost it when she said an all-girl gang.

That way, we won't get taken advantage of, you know? We won't have to put up with fuckin bullshit like that ever again. She was talking about my two-night stint as a hooker working for the Vipers, which, for the most part, I had blocked out of my mind.

But who will protect us?

We'll protect ourselves, same as always. She patted her lumpy coat pocket which held her new .32.

I don't know, Mac.

And I'll talk to my uncle about Lucifer's Choice backing us.

But, what if ...

What if what? Eh? What if we actually start seeing some real money from all the work we do? What if we get respect? What if we each end up driving a Lexus and living in an oceanfront mansion? Shit, I don't know, Mercy. At least we'll have tried. *We're gonna be the OGs, Merce*, she said in a whisper. I'll be the leader, and you'll be my right hand. No one would *dare* fuck with us.

What will we call ourselves?

The Roses.

The Roses?

What? You don't like it?

Nah.

Roses, as in roses that grew from concrete, you know, like Tupac wrote about.

Yeah, yeah, I get it, but it's too girly.

Mac took a swig of her Colt 45 and rolled her eyes. She flicked some stray hairs from her face, then took the elastic off her ponytail. Her roots had grown in, leaving a crown of dark brown hair, while the rest was bleached blonde, dry as dead grass. She needed a deep conditioning treatment. Bad. She ran her hands through her hair a few times, then gathered it up and put it back in a tight, smooth ponytail.

Okay, what should our name be then? she asked me.

How about, the *Black* Roses?

The Black Roses. She said it out loud a few times in different tones of voice, smacking her gum around in her mouth. Alright, I can live with that.

And so, on a rainy day in October, the Black Roses were born.

MAC

Mercy and I had been wracking our brains trying to come up with girls we could recruit. Unfortunately, everyone we came up with was an addict, a whore, or a square.

What about that tough chick from our elementary?

Which one?

That redhead, Kylie or Karla or something. Set the girls' washroom on fire that time? Used to wear safety pins in her ears? Always beating the shit out of people for no reason?

Oh, yeah, Kayla something. Had all those freckles.

Kayla O'Reilly.

She might be a good fit, if she's not a raging mental case by now.

Yeah, she was pretty intense.

Intense can be good, though. Do you know what she's up to?

Mercy shrugged. Heard she had a kid a couple of years ago. I've seen her around down here a few times, but she looks healthy enough.

Alright, well, next time we see her, we'll suss her out. See if she's what we're looking for.

What is it that we're looking for, exactly?

Bad bitches, I said, and lit my smoke.

Mercy laughed and reached for my lighter.

KAYOS

I sorta knew them from before, from back in the day, you know? I remember being at a couple parties they were at, a few years ago. They seemed like pretty cool chicks. I saw them around downtown sometimes and we said, what's up. You know, whatevs.

One day I was shopping on Granville and saw them walking with a case of beer. They called me over, asked me if I wanted to come back to their crib for pizza and beer. I said, sure. Why not, right? Their place was a run-down Vancouver Special on East Cordova. A total shithole, yo. Chain-link fence, scrubby brown grass, garbage in the driveway, junkies shooting up in the alley behind the house. Seriously. But they had their own place, all on their own, so whatevs, you know? And inside, it was actually pretty pimpin. Yeah, they'd done it up right. And so we're at their crib, shooting the shit, eating pizza, drinking beer; I'm admiring the cozy furniture, plush rugs, crazy-awesome paintings on the wall, wondering how they got all this sick shit. Then, they ask me if I want to be in their gang. I laughed.

I thought they were joking.

But they weren't. Uh, what do I have to do to get in?

Whatever you want.

What?

Whatever you think you need help doing.

Excuse me?

Look, what do you really want to do but feel like you can't do on your own? Mac asked. She stared at me with her laser eyes. She's super intense, right? She's not blinking, not moving, just drilling into me with those two green lasers, waiting for an answer.

That scene from *Psycho* flickered through my head. Me stabbing Roger. Blood spraying across the shower curtain. Of course, I couldn't tell them that. I couldn't tell anyone.

We had all gone to the same school, Lord Strathcona Elementary. They were a couple grades ahead of me. That was before Mom married Roger, and before we moved to Shaughnessy, back when we were still living in the Downtown Eastside. Mac and Mercy probably knew that I'd had a baby when I was thirteen. The funny thing was, I'd stayed in school. They hadn't. I didn't really know what they'd been up to since then. I'd heard somewhere that they were down with the Vipers, but I didn't know much else. Honestly, I felt honoured that they would ask me to join their gang. I mean, I just knew it was something I had to do. It was important. It was for real, yo.

I think they chose me because I had been sorta notorious in our school for getting in fights and blowing shit up, right? I've been working at developing my skills since I first got the shit kicked out of me by Wesley Gilditch in grade four. I work out five days a week at the gym, near our house. I take kickboxing and mixed martial arts. My mom wanted me to take ballet or figure skating or something lame like that, but my guidance counsellor told her kickboxing would be a good outlet for my aggression. So she bought me the deluxe gym pass that includes all the classes. I also have a weapons collection. Yo, want to know what's in it? Alright:

1 butterfly knife
1 switchblade
2 throwing stars
1 pair of brass knuckles
1 Samurai sword
1 BB gun
1 potato gun

Everyone collects something, right? It might as well be something cool. I picked most of it up at pawn shops or the Sally-Ann. I don't get many chances to use any of it. I fantasize about using my stuff all the time, though, mostly on Roger.

So I said carpe-fuckin-diem, yo, and joined the Black Roses. Something I'd always wanted was to get a tattoo. But I never had anyone to go with, and I'm only fifteen, so no one will give me one without parental consent, right? So the next weekend, me, Mac, and Mercy took the ferry over to Victoria and got black rose tattoos from Mac's Uncle Hank. He's a full-patch Lucifer's Choice and owns his own tattoo shop. How perfect, right?

You know about black roses? he asked us as he pressed the stencil onto Mercy's shoulder blade.

Just that they're about to bring the city of Vancouver to its knees, Mac said.

He chuckled, showing the black gaps where his canine teeth should've been. Maybe, maybe so. He cleared his throat and peeled back the plastic stencil sheet. In Medieval times, they said that whoever finds a black rose in the forest will be set on a path of liberation, the path of a freedom fighter.

Really? Cool.

It's also a symbol for anarchy, Mercy said. I looked it up.

And then Uncle Hank winked at Mercy, which was creepy cuz he's like fifty. But I guess he's kinda good looking for an old dude, plus he's L.C.

Mercy fluttered her doe eyes at him, and he turned on the tattoo machine. The buzzing sound filled up the room, and none of us talked for a minute or two.

Does it hurt? I asked Mercy.

Nah.

Tell the truth, Hank said, and stopped the machine to wipe away some inky blood that was dripping down her back.

Okay, maybe a little.

We all laughed at her.

He started the machine again. I have to put a lot of ink on this one because her complexion is so dark.

What, are you calling me brown?

We all laughed again.

How's your old man doing? he asked Mac after a while.

I don't know. Haven't heard from him in ages. She shrugged and started picking at her nails.

Then I remembered what I knew about Mac from back in the day at Lord Strath. Her dad was in jail, and her mom was a crack whore. I winced, remembering a day when kids threw rocks and garbage at Mac in the playground, called her a gutter slut, a jailbird. I had even thrown a few rocks myself, hiding behind the big yellow slide. I guess that's around the time she toughened up, became a bully, like me. Yo, me and Mac even fought once. Over something stupid, I don't remember what. An Adidas hoodie, I think. She gave me a bloody nose, I gave her a fat lip. But neither of us held a grudge, apparently.

Anyway, now Mac's uncle hooks us up with every connection we need. But we're not affiliated with L.C. at all. Nothing to do with them bikers. They just gave us a head start in the game, as Mac likes to say. But really, it's only because of them that we're allowed to deal in the Downtown Eastside.

My tattoo hurt like a bitch. I got it on my ankle so I could wear socks around the house and hide it from my mom. Yo, she'd shit on me if she ever saw it. It's really nicely shaded and almost looks like a real rose about to burst into full bloom. The petals are still a little bit closed. I love it so much. For real. Mac wanted hers on the back of her hand but her uncle persuaded her to go with the inside of her wrist instead. I guess she wants everyone to see it. Mac's was the biggest. About three inches across. It looks sick. Mercy's turned out super nice, too. Real dark petals, but still delicate and pretty.

After our tattoos were done, we smoked a joint with Hank, then he took us to an L.C. party at a penthouse in a swanky part of Victoria. It was a trip. Snow banks of blow, dude, seriously. I got really drunk and high and passed out early, but I know I was having hella fun up to that point.

I woke up in the morning in a huge waterbed with cotton-mouth and a raging headache. Mercy was on my left, snoring softly, and Mac was asleep on my right. That's when I knew, these were my girls, they were going to look out for me, they were going to keep me safe. No one has ever done that before.

Later that day, they asked me if I was ready to put in some work.

Sure, I guess.

We need some money, Mac said.

Uh-huh.

You're gonna get us some.

Okay…

It seemed like they had pulled this scam hundreds of times, and now they were testing me to see if I could handle it. To make sure I wouldn't fuck up, right? They laid it out for me step by step over lunch at the Noodle Box.

Only take out two or three hundred, Mercy said. Any more and it will raise flags.

Okay.

Any questions?

Who keeps the money?

We split it three ways.

Oh.

What? You don't think that's fair?

Well, since I'm the one doing it, I'm taking the risk, shouldn't I keep a bigger percentage?

Oh! Oh! See, you gotta change that way of thinking, girl! Mac rapped her knuckles against my forehead. You're running with the Black Roses now, right? We're a family, see? We *let* you keep a third of it, and the two of us get a third of it. Most crews, you just do the work and the OGs keep it all. One hundred percent. This here little group runs different. We're about equality and shit.

Mercy nodded, narrowing her amber eyes at me.

Okay, whatevs. Three ways is fine.

You sure?

Yep.

Because if you're not—

It's no problem.

Yeah?

It's cool, yo.

Good.

So, which bank should I do?

That's up to you. We finished our noodles and walked up Douglas; I stopped in front of the Scotiabank. I don't know why. Maybe because my favourite colour is red. When I was a kid, I used to think red Smarties gave me superhuman strength. Or maybe because there was a big, shiny killer whale statue out front, like it was a beacon or something.

Ready?

I nodded and pressed my tongue hard into the roof of my mouth.

Inside, two people were lined up at the ATM. My heart was hammering against my brain, and my hands were sweaty and shaky. The dude using the machine was tall with a black mohawk, the lady waiting behind him was a yuppie blonde wearing a Lulu tracksuit. I stood behind her, waiting, cracking my knuckles. When it was her turn, I watched her enter her PIN, repeating it in my mind. 1983. 1983. 1983. I've always had a terrible memory. I dropped a twenty on the ground by her feet. When she was collecting her cash, I cleared my throat. Uh, excuse me?

She whipped around.

Did you drop that? I nodded to the twenty.

Oh! She bent to pick it up and I grabbed her bank card out of the slot and popped in the fake one Mercy had given me. The machine beeped.

Shit.

Thank you so much! She smiled, tucking the money into her pink wallet. That was *so* honest of you. She grabbed the fake bank card and put it in her wallet without even looking at it.

No problem, I mumbled, and stepped up to the machine. I waited for her to leave, and then slid in her card. 1983. Savings. *How much? How much?* $300. And then, out it came. All fresh twenties, crisp and green.

Was that easy or what? Mercy grinned at me as I came out of the bank, squinting into the bright afternoon.

Yeah, I nodded. It was the most money I had ever held in my hands at one time. I shoved it into my purse and looked up and down the street, watching for cops, armoured guards, CSIS, whoever was coming for me.

Relax, girl. You're a natural, Mac said. She and Mercy laughed and held up their hands for me to slap them high-fives, and I did.

On the ferry back to Vancouver, we sat down at one of the little round tables in the cafeteria. We sipped iced tea and ate cherry Danishes that Mercy had stolen from the cooler.

These are disgusting, Mac said.

At least they were free.

They're not too bad, I said.

They both glared at me like I'd done something wrong.

Mercy finished her Danish and wiped her mouth on a napkin, then took a tube of lip gloss from her purse and reapplied. I think it's time, Mercy said.

Mac nodded, reached for her bag, and pulled out a sheet of paper covered in red ink. Read each rule out loud, she said, placing the paper on the table in front of me.

What?

Can you read?

Yeah. I looked down at the piece of paper. Obviously.

Read it, then.

....

Always honour and respect the Black Roses. Say/do nothing to defame any member or the gang as a whole.

Never rat on anyone in the Black Roses, no matter what has happened; death before dishonour.

Major decisions are group decisions. Always talk things over with other members before acting. In the event that the gang is divided, the final decision will be made by the leader, Mac.

All of Mac's decisions are final and cannot be contested. If Mac is unavailable, Mercy will step into her role.

Do not start shit with other crews. Violence and gang wars are useless and costly. If you have a problem with someone from another gang, talk it over with the Black Roses.

Everything you do is in the best interest of the Black Roses. Everything the Black Roses do is in your best interest.

Never call any of us by our real name. Never let anyone know your real name. We use our street names only.

Never bring anyone to Black Roses HQ without requesting specific permission ahead of time. Never let anyone know where Black Roses HQ is located.

Zero tolerance for drug consumption. If you are found to be using crack, cocaine, meth, or heroin, you will be ejected from the gang.

Love your Roses as you love yourself. No fighting within the gang, no backstabbing, lying, stealing, cheating, or scheming against fellow gang members. Stick together!

....

Can you agree to follow each and every one of these rules as they are written? Mac asked.

Yeah, I think so.

You think so? Or you can?

I can.

She raised her pale eyebrows and looked over at Mercy.

Mercy pursed her glossy lips, studied my face for a moment, then nodded.

Your new name is Kayos. Kayla doesn't exist anymore. You will be known only as Kayos from now on. Do you accept your new name?

Yes. I covered my grin with my hand and tried not to look

like a total moron. My whole face felt hot, and I blushed.

Now go memorize these rules by heart and come back when you're done.

Seriously?

Is that going to be a problem?

It's just that I …

What?

I, um, I'm really bad at memorizing stuff.

Well, here's a chance to challenge yourself. She shoved the list into my hand and turned away.

I looked at Mercy for help, but she was busy fiddling with her phone and waved me away without glancing up.

I found a quiet spot near the back of the ferry and curled up in one of the seats. I read the rules out loud over and over and then recited as much as I could from memory, whispering under my breath. It felt like it took about three hours, for real. But it couldn't have, because the whole voyage is only an hour and a half, right? I watched an old lady trip over somebody's guitar case, and a hippie-granola help her up. Then the chimes, and the announcement came on, *We are nearing the Tsawwassen Ferry Terminal. It is now time for all vehicle passengers to return to the vehicle decks.* My time was up. I would have to wing it, and if I fucked up, well, at least I had tried.

When I got back to their table, Mercy was painting her nails black, and Mac was reading the newspaper. They looked up at me standing there, and for a second, it seemed like they didn't recognize me.

Then Mercy snatched the sheet of paper away from me.

Alright, Kayos, let's hear the blood oath.

And then the worst thing that could have happened did. My mind went blank.

MERCY

She stood in front of us in the ferry's Coastal Café, all ready to recite the oath, and then this wave of redness spread up her neck and into her wide, freckly face, and it looked like she just fell apart inside. She looked so … empty. I wanted to help her, somehow. I looked at Mac. Mac looked at me. Kayos just stood there staring straight ahead, her big turquoise eyes getting all watery. Two little kids ran by our table, screaming, holding their paper cups like torches.

Let's go outside, I said. Too many people around here.

Alright, get to it, Mac said when we were all standing on the outer deck. She lit a cigarette and so did I. Kayos took a big breath, then began. She looked so nervous and unsure, just like that scared little fourth grade punk-ass kid we'd known her as. But she recited all the rules almost word for word, and I sort of felt like clapping at the end, but I didn't.

Good, Mac said. Now, sign your name to it. She pulled her jackknife from her back pocket and dropped it into Kayos's hand.

What? In blood? She laughed.

That's why it's called a blood oath, I said.

She stared at me for a second. Then she opened the knife and made a quick slit across her finger. She didn't even flinch; it was as if she'd done it a hundred times before. Mac and I smiled at each other as we flicked our butts over the side of the boat. Kayos wrote a big K at the bottom of the page in her blood.

Down for life? Mac asked.

Down for life. Kayos handed the paper to Mac, and Mac folded it neatly and slid it into her backpack. Then both of us gave Kayos a monster hug and told her she was our sister now, and we would love her and protect her forever.

SLY GIRL

I been livin in the Downtown Eastside bout six months by this point. Mostly on the street. Sometimes in squats, at tricks' places, once in awhile at a hotel if I could afford it. I seen these girls around, three of them. Always together, walkin fast, wearin all black. One was big and tall, a redhead, lookin some kinda tough, one had pale yellow hair to her shoulders, shark's eyes, a thin face, and the other one wore leather boots, big gold hoops in her ears, raven hair to her bum. She was a skinny Indian. Not Indian like me though, but Indian from India, eh. I knew these girls sold crack, H, and Oxy. Everybody knew that. Yeaah, I bought off them a few times. Their stuff was pretty good, but their prices...not the best.

I'd think on them girls sometimes, while I sat in the alley beside the Army & Navy Department Store, bout to shoot up or just on the nod, whatevers. Them girls would be rentin my headspace a lot of nights. I was curious about them. Who they were. What their story was. Who they were workin for. There ain't too many decent-lookin girls down here, if you know what I mean, so when you see some, you notice.

VANCOUVER

Puddles explode as heavy boots tramp through them. Neon lights reflect off my streets, off the water, off sharp, ever-scanning eyes. I've watched these three grow up; but they're not so old. I have watched them flip upside down on monkey bars, in a grassy park. I have seen them skin their knees and blow bubbles and make crowns of dandelions and necklaces of shells. I have seen their mouths fall open in wonder at the size of a tree, the vibrant violet of a sea star, a flock of geese stopping traffic on the bridge they call the Lions Gate. I have heard them tell their mothers they love them. But they don't do that anymore, they don't do any of that. Now they rob and steal and sell people their medicine. Their breath hangs silver in the air as they smoke cigarettes and walk fast—too fast— through these streets. My hardest streets. Where the people lie and cry and die in the alleyways, every single day. Did I know these girls would be here? Doing this? Maybe. But what could I do about it? What can I do but watch? And contain it all.

I know they still want to be loved. I know there is fear shining in the corners of their eyes. I know there are others who will become what they are.

my namez Z. ima graf wryter. graffiti iz aRt dEzyne <u>NOT</u> $treet cryme!!! my aRt iz all ova di$ citee & aLL up & doWn mayneland BC. u problee $een $uma my werk. bin throwin up Z, throwin up *i love you*, throwin up mad colorz all ova china-town all ova DTE$ cuz u know dem $ad a$$ junkie$ need $um colorz in der live$. dey need $um1 2 tell dem *i love you*. cuz tru$t me, ain't nobudee tellin dem. $o i make sum aRt 4 dem. cuz dey got real uglee live$, u know? i been approached by a few crewz. do Z wanna joyne dem? na uh. Z got her own thang goin on. i know dey ju$t wanna find out my $ecretz. Bcuz i can do mad upsyde downz, i get up in da Heaven $potz. dey $ay, grrl, dat $hit iz fre$h! dat is ri$kee bizness! howd u get up in dere? i say, how u think? cuz ima $tealthee a$$ muthafucka!!! lyke how i get up toppa billboardz, on monUmentz, trucks, trainz, & alla dat $hiznit. itz FUN. nobudee gonna fynd out my $ecretz tho. Na uh. Z workz alone.

i pict up my 1st $pray can when i wuz 12 & paynted my old $k8board. a year l8r i wuz catchin my 1st tagz, now my $tuff iz all ova. prolifik Z, dat$ me!

i kinda ran away frum hOme. i go back $umtimez @ nite when evrybudee's $leepin. i took off cuz i quit hi$kewl & den my parentz brainz XplOded. i quit $kewl cuz my teacherz $ed i can't be a graf aRti$t for a career. dey $ay dat$ no kinda career. $ame w/ da parentz. dey ju$t don't under$tAnd. dere lyke frum another planet or $um $hit. & my $i$terz R megAbitches. dey nevR leev me alone. call me a queer & a dyke & a boy &

awwwww fuck it. my parentz R alwayz tryin 2 set me up w/
dese chineze boyz. i tell dem, I DON'T LYKE BOYZ!!! but i
don't $ay it out loud. i yell it in$yde my hed in$ted.

i go out @ nyte, do my aRt, den go hOme & sleep & eat in
da daytyme when evrybudeez @ werk & skewl. itz aiight. 4
now. i don't wanna B a product of my eNvironment. i want my
eNvironment 2 B a product of me.

MERCY

We need some more members, Mac said. The two of us sat at our kitchen table smoking cigarettes, chopping crack. I'm sick of this shit.

What? Chopping?

Yeah, chopping. Chopping, cooking, inhaling these fuckin fumes. Dealing with dirty-ass junkies, fuckin crackheads and their fuckin dirty change, talking to pigs, standing out there on the corner getting drenched, risking our lives, all of it. All of it. You know?

Yeah.

We need someone who can be our narco girl. Someone who deals with all the prep and the running and slinging. Then *she* can be out on the corner all day while me and you go after the bigger fish, the cars, the ATMs, you know, the easy stuff. Instead of freezing our asses off all damn night to sell three-dollar rocks.

What about Kayos?

Nah, she don't know enough about it to do it alone. And she sticks out too much right now. She's a fuckin Shaughnessy chick, Merce, she'll get picked out in an instant. And you know what else? She ain't controlled enough to do it. Someone looks at her the wrong way out there, she'll fuckin curb stomp em. That'd be bad for business, know what I mean?

Yeah, I guess it would, I laughed.

We need someone chill. Street smart. You know anyone else? Anyone trustworthy?

Let me think. Someone trustworthy ... down here ... Nope. Not a soul.

I'm serious.

Me too.

She crushed her cigarette into the ashtray and glared at me.

Give me some time to think about it, I said. A few faces floated in my mind. A couple of hang-arounds I knew from the neighbourhood, some chicks I was in the group home with, but most of them were gone now.

She nodded, lit another smoke, and slid open the window beside her. Cold air rushed in and wrapped around my throat. Did you see that new mural in Blood Alley? Mac asked.

No.

Fuckin beautiful, man. Brilliant.

Oh yeah?

Yeah. The writer just signs it Z. Do you know who that is?

Nope.

I've seen some of his other work around. It's really good. I'm gonna see if I can find any of his stuff for here.

Really?

Yeah, it'd look awesome on one of these walls. Trust me.

It came as a bit of a shock to me that Mac had spent a chunk of our profits on original art. I never realized she was that into art, and I'd known her for seven years. Made me wonder how much there is to know about a person, and if you can ever really know anyone at all. Mac didn't draw or paint, but I think she secretly wanted to. We had repainted the house the month after we moved in, and she really got into choosing the colours. She had all these paint swatches lying around all over the house. She'd hold one up to the window and say something like, It looks different in the afternoon light. Or, does this colour remind you of blood or ketchup?

Both, I'd say, and walk out of the room, leaving her hunched over a hundred little squares of red.

The only room she didn't choose the colour for was mine. I painted it a deep purple. It was the exact same colour my room had been when I was little, living with my dad and brother in Surrey. My dad told me once that purple had been my mom's favourite colour, so then it became mine too. She died when I was three so I never really knew her. Hit and run. I remember the thick white lines of the crosswalk. Groceries all over the road. Then some stranger scooping me up and covering my eyes, and then I didn't see my mom ever again. My dad didn't talk about her much, so I had a hard time remembering her. We had fun in Surrey, though, me and Ranj and Dad. We were a good team, for a while.

Even though I knew those days were long gone, something about being in that purple room made me feel like a kid again, like magic existed and people were honest, and dreams could come true. Like the world was good and so was I. Stupid, I know.

Mac wrapped up the last packet of crack and reached for the piece of paper beside me. So, what's on the wish list this week? She read from it: An Escalade—black. A Lexus SC 430—white. A Porsche Cayenne—silver. Not bad. Wanna go pick them out later?

Sure.

Through Mac's Uncle Hank, we'd been hooked up with a car-theft ring run by Lucifer's Choice. They contracted us out and gave us a new list every two weeks. There were usually three to five cars on the list; model, make, colour, sometimes the year, although it was safe to assume all the buyers wanted this year's model. Then we'd cruise around the city in our little beat-up Honda Civic hatchback, smoke, listen to gangster rap, and find the cars.

Hank had put an app on my phone called OnStar. All I had to do was start the app within three metres of the car, and it would search through a series of coded number sequences. Once it found the right one, my phone would vibrate, and the car would unlock. Then I'd get in and start it with the keyless ignition button, or my nail file, if it didn't have one. Depending on how long the app took to locate the code, I could drive almost anything away in about five minutes. Too easy. And the cops never looked twice at me rolling in on my 24s, because I was just another Punjabi Princess, cruising in daddy's Beamer. I'd deliver the car to the port, and the dude at the parking booth would hand me a fat envelope. We made two grand per car.

If the car alarm went off or it was being a bitch to start, I'd say fuck it, and we'd go find another one of the same make. Sometimes we had to go out to Burnaby or Richmond to get the order, but not too often. Mac was good at spotting the cars, but she had never stolen one. Thieving was my thing.

I started when I was twelve, after my dad got killed in his cab. It started small: makeup, chocolate bars, magazines, junk like that. Then, when I lived at the group home, a girl there showed me how to line a shopping bag with tinfoil and boost whatever I wanted from any store in the mall. Then I'd get shitloads of CDs, designer clothes, shoes, jewellery, whatever, and sell it off at school or at the group home. I guess I haven't really paid for anything in about four or five years. But you better believe I'm the best-dressed PCP in East Van.

There's something about stealing... I don't know. I think it's good for me. I'm good at it. Really good. Maybe it's the only thing I can do really well, but at least it's something useful. Like when I'm doing a job, it's like nothing else matters, you know? And I don't think about people who have hurt me, or all the times I've fucked up, or my mom and dad being dead, or my little brother in foster care, or my friends who have died. I don't think about any of it. I'm just totally there, in that moment, taking something that doesn't really belong to anyone anyway.

SLY GIRL

One night I woke up, and there's a dirty-ass bum beside me with his fuckin hand down my pants!

Jesus Christ, man, at least pay for that shit. I pushed him off and stood up to zip my fly. And then I'm wonderin, why are my feet so cold? Look down and see someone stoled my shoes. Stoled my frickin shoes right offa my frickin feet! Oh, that's nice, I says. That's real nice.

You get to thinkin people are your friends out here, eh, you think people are watchin out for ya? They could give a fuck. Anyone and everyone will screw you over sideways if they think they can make a dollar off it. So I'm huntin around for somethin for my feet, it's raining, and it's a thin, cold rain that cuts right through your skin. It's still dark, and there's glass and rigs and shit all over the damn place. I need somethin for my feet. I'm goin through a dumpster and I find a grocery bag, eh, kinda heavy, maybe a little slimy. Could be somethin to eat, I think. My stomach's rumblin, all hungry and gettin excited. I open the bag. What's inside? A newborn baby, cold and grey. Its blank blue eyes starin straight up at me, all glassy like. Reminds me of this doll I used to have when I was a kid.

I dropped the bag and threw up on the pavement beside it. I walked and walked in the cold rain. Finally, I found a couple a garbage bags and some ripped up t-shirts in another dumpster, and I wrapped them around my feet. I walked around for the rest of the night in the freezin rain with these stupid dirty rags around my feet, just lookin for a fix or a bit of rock, a cigarette, just somethin, anythin, anythin at all. Because it's so cold and hard out here and I got nothin. Not even shoes.

I walked all night, no one would front me, no one would share what they had, and I had no cash cuz whoever took my shoes took alla that too. When the first light of morning burned through the clouds, I wandered down to the water and unwrapped my feet. They were bleedin and blistered, with bits of glass and stones stuck all in them and totally disgustin. I wanted to throw up again but there's nothin left in me to come out. I washed my feet in the ocean. Stung like a motherfucker. I could feel the junk sickness settlin down on me. It's heavy and dark, like a mean storm cloud. I knew then I needed some kinda change.

There's a drunk asleep on a bench in Crab Park. In his shoppin cart there's a pair of shoes. They're boy shoes, ugly as sin. They're a couple sizes too big for me, but they'll do. I didn't feel too bad about takin them cuz he already had shoes on, so he don't need them as bad as me.

I went back to workin the strip, but it's too early, there's no one around. Stood around a couple hours and finally got a trick, a BJ.

It's twenty, I said as he's puttin hisself back in his pants. He's skinny and red-faced, with a dick like a pencil.

He snorted. I'll give you five bucks.

But the price is twenty.

Yeah, but my dog is prettier than you, he said, and shoved a crumpled-up five into my hand, leaned over me to open the car door, then pushed me out onto the street and pulled away.

Does your dog give you blow jobs? I yelled after him. Pencil-dick prick!

I bought a three-dollar rock and smoked it to my head. Then the sky clears up and the sun comes out some and I feel like eating.

So I'm at the Carnegie, gettin a two-dollar lunch. A nice soup, a nice salad, nice bread. Then I see this little girl come in with her mom, little Native girl, and she's got her dolly swingin from one arm and she's holdin her mom's hand with the other, and she's gigglin and chatterin away and lookin up at her mom like ... like she's the only person in the wide world that matters. Her eyes all shiny and bright. Then suddenly, outta nowhere, I'm cryin into my soup. Just bawlin, eh. Like somethin inside me just broke, and I can't take another minute of bein who I am: livin on the street, turnin tricks, shootin junk and coke, smokin crack, smokin meth, stayin up all damn night so nobody climbs on toppa me. I mean, it's almost as bad as it was on the rez. I'm just so tired. I'm sick and I'm tired and my feet are bleedin and snot's drippin down my face into my soup and I don't even care. I let it drip. After awhile a fat white worker lady comes around and puts her hand on my shoulder and says, Do you want to go somewhere and talk, sweetie? And I *hate* that she calls me sweetie, cuz that's what some of them tricks call me. Even though I try never to think about them or remember them, I can't help seein some of their faces flash behind my eyes when she calls me sweetie. But how could she know that? And I *do* want to go somewheres and talk, away from all these grubby-ass, slobbery, stinkin bums, starin at my fucked-up face,

I do. I do. So, I do.

She takes me upstairs to a quiet little room full of books, and she gives me a hot mug of tea. It's black tea with milk and sugar, my favourite, and I love this fat white worker lady. I want to ask her to be my some kinda mom, and can I go home with her when she's done her shift at the Carnegie? I want to live at her house with her and I won't even get in her way, I promise I won't. I can sleep in her closet, and she won't even have to worry on me because I will be good. I will be so good and never make a mess or get high or have boyfriends over or anything. I'll just stay out of her way and sleep in the closet and drink tea.

When I'm calmed down enough to talk, I tell her I need a change. I want to get off the street. I want to get off the drugs.

She nods like that's exactly what she was expectin me to say. How old are you, hon?

Thirteen.

Well, the good news is there's a lot of help out there for you if you're ready for it.

I nod, gulp my sweet milky tea. It doesn't burn me, it doesn't burn. It's okay. Everythin's gonna be okay. I start cryin again and she hands me a box of Kleenex. I want to ask her to be my mom, but I don't.

VANCOUVER

The blue-black night folds into me, and the people of my city search for sleep. Some find it on waterbeds, futons, goose down feather mattresses; others in parkades, stairwells, dark doorways, shining alleys. Still others don't look for sleep at all, but something else entirely. Something necessary and familiar. They hunt through the night, bleary-eyed, fervent, skin glowing green under the buzzing streetlights, moaning into the wind like hungry ghosts.

One day, around Christmas, I was weighing out baggies when Mercy burst through the front door, all excited and grinning.

I found her, she said.

Found who?

Our runner. Our narco chick.

Oh yeah? Who is it?

Little Native girl from the neighbourhood. We used to sell to her, long time ago. She's got kind of a fucked up face …

Wait a sec, we used to *sell* to her? Fuckin forget about it.

But—

No way, Mercy. No fuckin way. No junkies. No crackheads. No tweakers. No fiends. No way, no how. Come on, what the hell are you thinking? You know how they are. We're trying to run a business here!

She's six weeks clean.

Whoop-dee-fuckin-doo. That don't mean jack shit.

Well, she's got the right background. She knows her shit. She knows all the customers already, and she's smart.

How do you know?

Because you don't last on the street if you're stupid.

I shook my head. Not happening.

She blinked her eyes a few times and pouted. I wondered if she was wearing fake eyelashes. Then she came around behind me and started rubbing my shoulders. She smelled like salt water and cinnamon. Come on, Mac. She'll be good for us. Let's give her a chance.

No, Mercy! Forget it. I pushed her hands away.

I couldn't believe she would even suggest bringing an addict into the Black Roses. It would destroy everything we'd worked so hard to build. She didn't understand that six weeks clean meant fuck all—hell, six months, too. I'd grown up with an addict. She hadn't.

Sometimes I would feel like a normal little kid. Mom would go straight for a while and get her welfare cheques sent directly to our landlord so she wouldn't be tempted to buy coke and heroin with the money. She'd make macaroni and cheese or scalloped potatoes, and we'd sit on the couch and drink Ovaltine and watch *Sally Jessy Raphael* or *Geraldo*. She'd call me her princess and braid my hair, make sure I brushed my teeth, tuck me in at night, and read me stories from the *National Enquirer*. Those were the good times, the times I hoped would last forever. But then it would rain for six days in a row, or something I did would piss her off, and she'd get restless. Then she'd say, I'm just going out for some smokes, honey. And she'd be back out on Hastings. Gone for two, three, twelve days at a time. She's still out there, far as I know. Either there, or rotting in pig shit out in PoCo. I haven't seen her in about four years. I don't even know if I'd recognize her if I did see her. I know it sounds stupid because she's a crack whore and everything, but sometimes, I miss her. I really do.

SLY GIRL

Turns out the well-dressed Indian girl's name is Mercy. She invited me over to her place for Christmas dinner tomorrow night. I almost cried when she did, cuz it's my first Christmas on the street and everythin, and for the past week and a half it was like God took a fat, slushy shit on the whole world. When she came up to me, I was freezin and hungry, and all the tricks had gone home to their wives for the holidays. It was the nicest thing anyone could've done for me right then. I decided to stay straight too, cuz I didn't want to make a fool of myself in front of them girls. I'd told Mercy I'd been clean for awhile. Which was sorta true, cuz I hadn't been doin hardly nothin at all, and I'd gone through detox and everythin. Man, I'll tell ya, that was some kinda nightmare. Then, after detox, they put me in a group home while I waited for a foster home. But it didn't work out. Story of my life, eh. Ha ha.

Well, I couldn't wait around with all them crazy chicks for six to twelve weeks, or however long it was gonna take to get a foster place lined up for me. Jeez, some of them girls were brick shithouse insane. It was too much to have to sleep beside them, eat with them, talk to them. They were all fucked up. And I know I'm not perfect, but these chicks made me look like an angel. I thought this one girl was gonna kill me! Serious. Nasty white chick. She liked my jeans. Then she liked my lipstick. She said maybe somethin bad would happen to me, then she could have all my stuff. This other girl said she could make it so my right eye matched my left, and showed me this rusty steak knife she kept under her pillow. Said she could do it while I was sleepin, so I wouldn't feel nothin. Crazy bitch. So I took off. And now here I am, back out on the street. Just tryin to make it through, one day at a time.

MERCY

I didn't think Mac would let Sly Girl into the gang, but I had to try anyway. I don't know why. Something about this girl … stopped me. I felt like she needed us. She needed the Black Roses, and we needed her. Just one of those feelings you get sometimes about a person. You ever get that?

So I brought her over for Christmas dinner. Kayos couldn't come because she was feasting with her family somewhere in Shaughnessy, but she said she'd sneak out later and come over. Mac and I had nowhere to go, and I thought it would be kind of lonely with just the two of us, so I brought Sly Girl over and made mashed potatoes and butter chicken. I could tell by the way she ate that she lived on the street, but it didn't really matter to me. I knew she would be good for us. And I knew she'd be good at selling our shit on the corners. She already knew who was who and what everyone's poison was and what they would be prepared to pay. I mean, she would probably be better at it than me and Mac. As long as she stayed sober. And I doubted that anyone out there would fuck with her because she looked so scary. Her left eye and cheek were all disfigured. Like she'd been in some kind of accident, or attacked by a dog or something. She told us she was from an Indian reserve in Alberta. I figured her scars were from something that had gone down there. She said she was never going back. She said the Downtown Eastside was a kind of heaven compared to that place. At least people look out for you here, she said, and shoved a forkful of potatoes past her lips.

I looked at Mac. She had hardly said anything all night. She took a big gulp of her wine.

Ask her, I mouthed across the table.

Mac and I watched Sly Girl as she swallowed without chewing and shovelled more and more potatoes into her mouth, until they were all gone and she reached for seconds.

So, you get high? Mac asked.

Nah, not no more. I used to, but you know, I gotta make it to fourteen. She laughed, put her hand to her face, covering her bad eye.

I nodded at Mac.

So, what is it you all do for work, if you don't mind me askin? She drained her wine glass and I poured her another.

We're in a gang, Mac said. An all-girl gang.

Really?

Yeah.

That's cool.

Wanna be in it?

Hells yeah, she said. And just like that, we had our runner.

I grinned at Mac and Sly Girl, and raised my glass in a toast. To the Black Roses. May we have everything we need, and get everything we want.

KAYOS

New Year's Eve was busy on the street because everyone wanted to party harder than they usually do, which, as you can imagine, is really fucking hard. After dinner, Mac had sent me out with Sly Girl to work the corners. It was nasty out there with the wind and sleet, not to mention all the strung-out freakshows skittering around on their wobbly legs. I hated it, for real. But Mac said Sly Girl needed someone out there with her, to make sure she felt safe. Soon she would get her own gun, and then maybe I wouldn't have to go with her anymore. Honestly, yo, I think I was just there to make sure she didn't make off with the stash or smoke what she was supposed to be selling. I kinda just stood back in the shadows and let her make all the transactions. She was doing good. She was quick and subtle enough about it all, and as far as I could tell, she was sober as a nun. I knew she'd had problems with drugs, but who hasn't? I mean, this is the Downtown Eastside. You're a product of your environment. Probably the only reason I'm not an addict is because I got pregnant before I could really get a taste for it, then we moved to Shaughnessy, and, well, it wasn't around so much.

As I was thinking about all this, this fucking guy with a huge tarantula tattooed on his neck comes up to Sly Girl. He gets all in her face, right, and starts yelling, *What the fuck you doin, bitch? Don't you know this is Unified Peoples territory?! Get the fuck outta here!* Go on, get your ugly ass outta here, you skanky pirate hooker. Go back to whore island! *Git!*

Sly Girl lowered her head and started to walk away, but I

stopped her and closed my fist around the handle of the .32 inside my jacket pocket.

Hey fuck-ass, listen here, I said to the guy. We've got just as much right to be out here as you do, so you better step off, *bitch*.

He spat on the ground and a fat wad of phlegm landed beside my foot.

Oh yeah? He stepped toward me.

Yeah.

You're one crazy bitch. Who you claimin?

The Black Roses, don't mess.

He started to laugh. That pussy gang? I heard of yous. I thought yous was a joke! Yous are for real? That's hilarious! Then he stopped laughing. You know what? If you had any brains in that head of yours, you'd back on outta here right fuckin now. Take your girlfriend here, and never come back. Unified Peoples control the Downtown Eastside, and anyone who says different gets a face-to-face meet with Mr Smith and Mr Wesson, know what I'm sayin? His pocket bulged with what must have been his gat.

Inside I was shaking, but I knew I couldn't back down to this fuck-wad or I'd permanently ruin the name of the Black Roses. This was my job, to represent.

Listen, fool, we're here. We've got loyal customers. We're not leaving. Deal with it.

He stepped closer to me, the veins in his neck bulging under the spider.

The market's big enough for both of us, don't you think? I

glanced right and left into the alleys beside us, where junkies scuttled through the night like rats.

His dark eyes flashed with a meanness that made me want to run as fast and as far as I could.

Bitch, you and me's got beef now. You're lucky I'm on probation, or I'd knock your head off right here, right now, I swear to God.

I turned to Sly Girl. Whaddya think, Sly?

She shrugged, retreating into her hoodie like a turtle into its shell.

I guess we'll take a walk over to Oppenheimer, offload the rest of this quality shit. We turned away from him and started walking.

Don't even think about it! Oppenheimer's ours too! You can fuck off outta here! Hear me?

We kept walking. Every hair on the back of my neck was standing up. I expected a bullet to rip through my spinal cord at any second. But he didn't shoot. He just kept yelling.

This was your warning! You only get one!

I looked at Sly Girl. Her messed-up eye was twitching like crazy. I guess she has a nervous tic or something. I stopped when we got around the corner and lit a smoke. I handed it to her, then lit another for myself.

What the hell was that? she asked.

That was fucked up. That's what that was.

Sheesh.

I should've shot him, I said. My hand shook as I flicked my ash. I should've fucking shot him.

No.

Yes!

Just take it easy, Kayos. Nobody's shootin nobody. We're gonna go talk to Mac, see what she has to say about all this. Come on, let's go back to the house. Besides, we need to re-up anyways.

I can't believe that fucking guy. Who the fuck does he think he is?

He's Unified Peoples.

So?

So, they're pretty big, you know. They've got property, I guess.

That's just as much our property as it is his, yo.

She shrugged.

Fuck! I kicked a car tire.

She giggled. Hey, Kayos?

What?

Are you down with OPP?

Huh?

I said, are you down with OPP?

Yeah, you know me.

MERCY

Kayos's knees vibrated as she sat on the couch, telling us what had gone down.

So, what did you say? Mac asked her.

I said we've got just as much right to be down there as he does, and he'd better just step off.

Did he touch you?

No. She looked at Sly Girl

Did he touch *you*?

No.

Good.

But he said that was our only warning.

Fucker.

We all looked at each other. Sly Girl's eye was twitching. She and Kayos were both restless, fidgety.

You didn't say anything about L.C. backing us? Mac asked.

No.

Why not?

I don't know. Is that everybody's business?

Well, it's gonna make it so nobody fucks with us. So yeah, I wouldn't keep it a secret.

Wouldn't they already know that because of where we were, though? Kayos asked.

You know what we need, ladies? I said.

What?

We need a publicist.

Mac raised an eyebrow at me.

You know, someone who's going to get our name out there. Let all the other crews know we're the real deal, and they can't just tell us to screw off because there are going to be consequences.

I don't know, Merce, Mac said. Do we really want to be exposing ourselves like that? I thought we were gonna keep a low profile. Stay out of all the colours and kid's stuff.

You mean like tags and shit? Kayos asked.

Yeah, tags, but more than that, big pieces too. What we need right now is some street cred. We're like a brand, right? We have to get our brand name out there. Then we get more customers, more respect and—

More attention from cops.

Aw, *fuck* the police. Cops never look twice at girls. Do you have any idea all the criminal shit I've pulled? All the B & Es, all the frauds, the stolen goods—thousands of dollars of shit. Have I ever once been arrested? Detained? Hell, I've never even had a speeding ticket. If the cops get on us about anything, it's for suspicion of prostitution, but it's not illegal to be a prostitute, it's illegal to procure a prostitute's services, and obviously we're not pimps, so they can get fucked.

They laughed.

So, did you have anyone in mind for this *publicist role?* Mac asked.

Yeah, actually.

Who?

Your girl, Z.

Hold up a minute, we don't know if Z is a girl or a guy.

Well, word on the street is she's a girl. Little Chinese girl.

Really?

True story.

How'd you find that out?

I've got connections…

Mac rolled her eyes. She'd been sitting at home, making crack, counting our money, watching TV, and learning to paint with Bob Ross all month, so she was kind of out of the loop.

I don't know, Mercy. I'll have to think about it, she said.

Well, while you're thinking about it, I'll set up a meet.

Whatever, she walked out of the room. I hoped she was going to wash the dirty dishes she'd left on the counter for three days.

Yo, do you guys mind if I crash here tonight? Kayos asked. I think I missed the last train. She ducked her head as if she was expecting me to smack her.

Kayos, I said. You're a Black Rose. This is your place too, okay? You can stay here whenever you want, you don't have to ask anybody. You have a key, right?

Yeah.

As long as you never bring anyone here, or tell anyone where we live, you can come and go as you please.

Alright, cool. Thanks.

We heard an enormous burp from Mac's room and we all giggled. I took out my silver cigarette case and offered smokes around. Some drunks in the street were hollering, then singing, and then we heard glass being smashed in the road.

You can sleep in my room if you want, Sly Girl said. It's quieter in there.

Oh, that's okay. I'm fine on the couch.

Sly Girl shrugged and went into the bathroom.

Kayos cracked the knuckles of each hand.

Are you okay?

Yeah, yeah, I'm good. Just shook me up a little, you know. I was getting ready to pull out my piece, Mercy, she whispered. For real.

Well, I'm glad you didn't.

But, I mean, I would have. If I'd had to.

I know.

my frend Ben-E tellz me de$e chix wan2 meet me. Them's good people, he $ez. You should see what they want.

realee? ur not fuckin w/ me, ryte?

No way!

OK. tell dem i $ed OK.

$o we meet @ da coffee shop across frum Victory Square. wen i walk in dere$ de$e 4 hardCORE lookin chix $ittin in lo chairz by da wyndO. dey $tand up wen i cum ovr. blond 1 $tepz 2wdz me & $tix out her hand. Hi, I'm Mac. her $myle iz quick lyke lightning & $he is da most BeaUtiFUL grrl i have evR $een in my hole lyfe. 4reaL. 4 a minute, i 4get my own name.

Z, i $ay, finalee.

& dere$ dat $myle again. I've seen your work around town, it's really good, $he $ez.

Thanx. my face iz on FYRE! $he likes my werk! $he realee lykes it! i'm lookin @ de$e chix thinkin, wat cood dey po$$iblee want frum me? den i reaLyze, i don't care wat dey want, i'll do it. az long az i get 2 C her again.

Do you want a coffee? da brown chick sez.

$ure, a latte.

K. $he hedz 2 da counter.

$o watz all di$ about?

Well, Mac $ays, we were wondering if you're with a crew?

na, Z fliez $olo.

Would you consider joining one?

OK so dere recrUtin me 4 a $pray cru, problee want a lookout.

i get it. dependz, i $ed.

On? da left corner of her mouth iz tuRnin up & reVealin a dimpL in her cheek. evN tho i'm melting in$yde, i'm playin it cool.

on wat i hafta do. watz in it 4 me?

brown chick cums bak w/ lattes 4 evrybudee & $etz em down.

thanx.

No problem. $he $itz down & $tartz talkin. What we're here to ask you today, Z, $he $ez, is if you would consider joining us.

& who R U?

We are the Black Roses. Have you heard of us?

na. wat R U? a new graff cru?

dey look @ eachoder. No, $ez Mac. $he leanz clo$R 2 me & my neez tingle. We're a criminal organization.

wat?

A gang.

O.

Yeah.

U mean lyke U.P. & Vipers & $hit?

Right.

nevR herd of U.

Well, that's the problem we're hoping you'll help us solve, brown chick $ez. We want a public presence; we want our name thrown up all over the city.

Y?

Because writing our name on the walls tells the world we're here, and they can't ignore us. With all their boundaries and their sanctions and their rules and laws, with all their money and power, we're still here. And we're not going away. Our name on the wall proves it.

Y don't U ju$t do it ur$elve$. Y do U need me?

Because you're the best, Mac $ed.

i coffed in2 my hand 2 hyde my grin.

Mercy arranged a meet with this Z person. I told everyone they had to come. I wanted her to know who we were, that she was getting the unique opportunity to become one of us.

So we're all sitting in the comfy chairs in the corner of Bean Around the World, watching people pass by the window doing the Hastings shuffle.

What if she doesn't want to join us? Kayos asked. She will.

Is she gonna live with us? Sly Girl asked.

Yeah, if she wants.

Where will she sleep?

We'll figure something out.

There were only three tiny bedrooms in the ratty house we rented on Cordova, but I was saving up so we could get a condo uptown, something real nice. A bright home with lots of windows, a balcony, maybe even a view of the mountains. Something far, far away from the hellhole that is the Downtown Eastside. Sometimes it feels like I've been waiting my whole life to get out of here, and for the first time, I'm actually getting close.

And let's agree on something, I said and looked at each of them. If she wants in, this is the last member of the Black Roses. We can't have this thing getting too big, you know? Or it'll get out of control. We'll just keep it to five members, max. That way, everyone knows each other really good, we know we can trust each other, and we can all live together. Agreed?

Yeah, sure.

Okay.

Agreed.

Good.

The other reason I didn't want more than five people was because we weren't making enough profit yet to support any more than that and afford a condo. One day soon, I wanted to drive a sweet car, a Corvette or a Porsche. I wanted a diamond choker, and a floor-length leather jacket. I wanted a little dog to carry around in my purse and dress up in little outfits. Just kidding, I didn't really want a pocket rat, but you get the picture. Feeding, clothing, and housing another girl would seriously cut into my bling funds.

I didn't feel comfortable managing a huge crew; some people could do it, but never for long. The big street gangs always get taken down, either by mutiny or the cops. I wanted this to stay small and highly efficient. I wanted to be organized. I wanted to be tight. And I wanted each member to be able to reap big rewards, instead of spreading it thin across a bunch of girls. As I was thinking this, a scrawny Chinese girl walked up to us. She was not what I expected a graffiti artist to look like. She had spiky black hair, thick glasses, and Adidas warm-up pants. She was cute as hell.

I stood up first, and everyone else followed my lead. I extended my hand to her. Hi, I'm Mac. Her T-shirt said *Support Your Local Hustler*. I couldn't help smiling.

She looked like she swallowed her gum the wrong way, and

her eyes got huge and watery behind her glasses.

You must be Z.

Yup. She coughed into her hand and I let mine drop back to my side.

This is Mercy, Kayos, and Sly Girl.

She wrinkled her nose like she smelled something bad.

Won't you sit down? I heard myself say. Jesus Christ, who am I, Martha Stewart? Why am I nervous? This chick's like, four feet tall. Mercy, would you mind grabbing us some coffees? I slid her a fifty.

Sure, what do you want? she asked Z.

A latte?

I'll have the same.

Me too, said Sly Girl.

Me three, said Kayos. And could you get them to make mine a triple, please? I don't know why I'm so tired today. She yawned and stretched.

Someone keeping you up late last night? Mercy winked.

No. Kayos glared at her.

So ... I said.

So? Z set her backpack on the floor and I heard the metallic clink of what must've been spray cans inside.

You live around here?

Yup.

Chinatown?

Yeah, all Chinese people live in Chinatown. Didn't you know?

Sorry, I didn't mean ... it's just that it's around here ... and ... sorry. Shit, this was not going well. She was so small and so cute. She was such a great artist, she was a perfect fit for us, and I was screwing up everything.

We're not racist, Kayos said. Obviously. She gestured to Mercy standing in line.

Whatever.

Do you, um, do you get high?

What are you, a narc or something? You undercover? Fuck this shit, man. She picked up her bag and stood to leave.

No, no! No, God, no. Please, sit down. I put my hand on her shoulder and felt a little electric shock zap me. I'm sorry. It's just that I have to make sure before ...

She sat down with a huge sigh. So what's all this about?

Well, I said. We were wondering if you're with a crew.

No way. Z is a one-woman show.

Would you consider joining one?

Depends.

On?

On what's in it for me and what I have to do. She tilted her head and stared at me as if I were her mortal enemy.

I smiled. Z was a tough nut to crack.

Mercy came back with our coffees and sat down.

I gave Mercy the nod to go ahead and take over. Like my mom used to tell me, if you don't know what to say, shut the hell up and let someone else do the talking.

Mercy gave her the spiel about who we were and what we did, and if she was with us, she'd have to be okay with it all. She'd have to promote the Black Roses through her art. In return, she would get our protection, a place to live, an equal share of the profits, and, of course, our undying love.

I'll think about it, Z said, and stood up.

I felt a sudden pain ripple through my chest. Wait. I wrote my cell number on a napkin. Take this.

She snatched it out of my hand and was gone.

Mercy, Kayos, Sly Girl, and I were left staring at each other and shrugging our shoulders.

Whaddya think? Kayos said.

I don't think she's into it, said Mercy. I don't think we have anything she wants.

She already talks like a G, anyway. She's part way there, yo.

Sly Girl giggled.

I guess we'll have to wait and see, I said, and finished the dregs of my coffee. As I set my mug down, a cold rush of air blew in. Z came through the door and rushed up to us, all breathless and rosy-cheeked.

Okay. I thought about it. I'm in.

VANCOUVER

These girls?

These girls are like five sudden stars, exploding into the night.

SLY GIRL

I was still workin the streets, just in a different way. Now, I was selling H, crack, and Oxy instead of blow jobs, hand jobs, and pussy. The streets were still hard and nasty, but at least I wasn't sleepin on them no more. And I always went out with another Black Rose, usually Kayos, sometimes Mac or one of the others. It's not that they didn't trust me to do it myself, it's just that they didn't want me to be alone out there, in case some crackhead got violent or somethin, you know.

I'd stopped doin meth and heroin, but every now and then I took a few hits of crack. Just because it was everywhere, and it was easy and free. I was scared that Mac would catch me, but I hid it from her real good.

What I would do is, I'd smoke a teensy, tiny little rock in the dead middle of night. Around three or four in the morning I'd just take my pipe outta my hidin place and have a little hit. Blow it all right out the window. Once, I was this close to gettin busted by Z. She got home right as I finished. She was the only one who stayed out that late usually, sprayin up the town with our name. I wanted to go with her real bad, eh, but she said she preferred to work alone. Whatevers. She's nice enough. Doesn't get in my way or stare at my ugly eye. Her and Mac share Mac's room.

Kayos and I like to work in the daylight cuz then you can see who's comin. One afternoon, we were out, must've been around two or three. I'm makin a deal with Cindy, one of our regulars at the corner of Hastings and Columbia. Kayos is havin a cigarette, checkin out some of the kiff beside us. Then outta nowhere, our buddy with the spider tattoo on his neck comes chargin around the corner. He's all huffin and puffin. *What the fuck did I tell you bitches?* He yells at us. *Stay the fuck outta U.P. territory!* Then he reaches into his pocket, but Kayos reaches into hers first, and fires off a shot at him. And then another. And then another. It's so loud right beside my ear. My ears are ringin and hurtin bad, and he is bleedin from the heart, and staggers toward us with his arms reachin out for us. Then he falls to the ground. I look at Cindy and her mouth forms a giant O, and she runs down the street, her arms and legs all jerky like a chicken.

Come on! Kayos grabs my arm and pulls me down the alley, and we run and run and run and run and run until we're at our house on Cordova and in the front door. Kayos locks and bolts and chains the front door, and her hands are shakin so much she has trouble with the chain. When we turn around, Mac and Z are starin at us. They're eatin sandwiches, and Mac finishes chewin and swallows and takes a drink of milk before she says, What the hell did you do?

KAYOS

Hey! Mac yelled and snapped her fingers in my face. What the fuck just happened?

I sat on the floor with my back against the door and Mac, Z, and Sly Girl stood over me. I pulled out a smoke and tried to light it, but I couldn't get my lighter to work. I tried again and again, but it just wouldn't. Finally, Mac flipped her Zippo in my face and lit it for me. I took a long, hard drag.

I think I just killed someone.

What? Who?

That U.P. guy we told you about, who harassed us the other night.

You shot him?

I took another big drag, held it in. Nodded. Exhaled.

Oh, *fuck me*, Kayos! Do you realize this is gonna fuck us up royally? This is exactly the kind of shit I didn't want us to be involved in. *Fuck!!!* She grabbed her forehead. What happened? Tell me exactly what happened.

It was self-defence, yo. I swear. He charged at us, he was yelling, and then he went for his gun. He was gonna execute us right there on the corner! We'd both be dead right now if I hadn't got to mine first. Right, Sly?

She nodded.

Sirens screamed a few streets away.

This is fucked up, Mac said.

Z rubbed her hand over Mac's back. Just chill out, girl. We gotta stay calm right now. Let's all take a deep breath, aiight?

Okay. We're not gonna panic. We're all gonna be smart right now. Okay? Everybody smart? Yeah, that's right.

Did anybody see you?

Sly Girl nodded.

Who?

Cindy, I said.

Who else?

I don't know! Whoever was standing around at Hastings and Columbia right then. Probably lots of people!

Christ.

What do you want me to do? I asked her.

I want you to go back in time and *not fucking shoot him!!*

I looked down. I had fucked up everything. For real. I'd broken the oath, I'd probably started a gang war, and I had let everyone down. I began to cry.

Then there was pounding on the door behind me, which scared the living shit out of all of us.

Hey! Let me in, it's Mercy!

Is anyone with you? Mac yelled through the door.

No.

Move. Move! Mac shooed me away from the door and unlocked it for Mercy. She burst in smelling like pine air freshener. Hey, good news, I just loaded this Escalade onto the ... What's wrong?

Kayos shot a guy from Unified Peoples.

Oh. *Shit.*

MERCY

Look, Kayos, I said, I think the best thing for you to do right now is go home and be with your family. Go have dinner with them. Stay in. And make sure they stay home with you tonight. Play Monopoly or something.

She rolled her eyes and wiped the tears from her face.

Come on, I'll give you a ride home.

I grabbed her arm and pulled her up off the floor. All the colour had drained out of her face, and she'd chewed her lower lip so hard it was bleeding.

I'm sorry. I—

Hey, it's going to be alright. Black Roses stick together.

I'm really sorry, she whispered.

I put my arms around her and squeezed, then motioned with my hand for the other girls to join us. At first they hesitated, but after a minute we were all in a big clump, hugging Kayos and each other.

Bad bitches don't die, I said. And they all repeated me in unison.

On the way to her place, we passed a ghost car, and she ducked low in her seat and pulled her hood up over her head.

How old are you again?

Fifteen.

Right. Well, hey, worst-case scenario, you get caught and go to juvie for a year. It's no big deal, not like it's hard time or anything, it won't even go on your permanent record.

Really?

Hey, don't worry, okay? We don't even know if he died or not yet.

Mercy—

What?

I shot him three times in the chest.

Hm. I stopped at a red light. Drummed my fingers against the steering wheel.

She lit a cigarette and rolled down the window. Motherfucker was headed to an early grave anyway, she said. Seriously. Thinking he can fuck with us? Fuck that gutter scum. She spat onto the road.

I stifled a little laugh. What could I say? The girl was tough.

Yo, I'm not saying he deserved it, but he probably did. He probably killed tons of people already, and he was about to kill me and Sly Girl next. I mean, I did the right thing. Right?

I stared at the glowing stoplight.

Right?

Yeah, I nodded. You did.

When I pulled up in front of Kayos's house, I got a small shock. You live *here?* I whistled through my teeth. *Damn*, girl. You've been holding out on us.

The house was a three-storey, three-car garage monstrosity with fancy-ass landscaping, a fountain, marble lions, the works. It looked like it belonged on the cover of a magazine. I sat staring at the house; it was practically a mansion. If she lived here, what the hell was she doing slumming it with us on the Downtown Eastside?

Thanks for the ride. She slung her backpack over her shoulder and slammed the car door.

Hey! I leaned over to the passenger window and called after her. Be good!

She rolled her eyes. Right.

I motioned for her to come back over to the car. Just lay low for awhile, okay? Stay here. Don't come downtown. This'll all blow over in a few days.

But—

We'll call you when it's safe to come back.

Okay. She bit her lip.

Later.

I pulled away from the curb, glancing in the rear-view to see her give me a limp wave.

SLY GIRL

After Mercy and Kayos left, I went into my room and shut the door. I sat down on my bed and just started shakin. I felt like I was gonna throw up. And then, I did. I threw up on a towel, then rolled it in a ball and shoved it in the back of my closet. I just couldn't deal with it right then.

Kayos shooting that U.P. guy somehow brought it all back, everythin I thought I forgot—everythin I been tryin so hard and long to block out—flashed in front of my eyes like I was seein it all again on a movie screen.

I seen a lotta crazy shit on the rez. I seen my cousin Bo get shot in the belly and bleed to death in my kitchen. I seen my brother Lenny get shot in the shoulder, the red flesh all ripped up like the inside of a fish. I seen Lenny stab a guy by the basketball courts, stab him in the neck with a broken beer bottle. I seen my brother, Eugene, get shot in the back, get paralyzed for life over a fifty-dollar debt. I seen one of my mom's boyfriends smack her across the face with his gun because she smoked his last cigarette. I seen my brother Neil push his girlfriend down the stairs so she wouldn't have her baby. I seen the cops bash my brother's hands with clubs until all his fingers were broken and hanging from his hands like bloody sausages. I seen my mom threaten to kill my uncle with an axe. I seen my cousin shoot a dog in the head with a .22. I remember my uncle Leo stickin his gun up my asshole, makin me tell him I liked it. Then stickin it in my mouth. Askin me if I wanted him to pull the trigger. Yes, I'd nod, gaggin on the gun. Yes. Do it. Just do it. Please. And I meant it.

Then he would.

Click.

The gun would click inside my head so loud, but the chamber was empty, and I still wasn't dead.

But you know I wanted to be.

I remember gettin shot in the face. Knowin that my whole life was blown apart at that moment. Knowin that now I didn't stand a fuckin chance.

I got out my pipe and smoked a fat rock, then lay down on my bed and tried to stop shakin. I closed my eyes and let the hot tears slide down my face. It was all I could do.

Later, Mac knocked on my door. I was afraid she had smelled the crack burnin and was gonna kick me out, but when she came in, she didn't seem mad.

You okay?

I nodded, wiped my nose on my sleeve.

She sat down on my bed. You ever see someone get shot before?

Yeah, I said. Too many people.

She nodded. After a minute she wrinkled up her nose. It kinda smells weird in here…

I puked, I said.

Oh.

Yeaah.

Is there anything I can do for you, Sly Girl? Do you want some tea or soup or something?

I looked down at my dirty nails. I dunno.

I'm gonna make you some chamomile tea. It soothes the nerves. Okay? She put her hand on my shoulder and I flinched.

Okay.

Alright. She closed the door quietly behind her and I could hear her and Z whisperin in the hallway. I was glad they were there. I was glad I didn't have to do everythin alone no more.

I've never thought of myself as a lesbian. Never pictured myself in a relationship with a woman. Only ever been with men. All of them stubborn, selfish—still boys, really. I'd thought of dykes as weak and kind of nasty, actually. But then I met Z. And the truth is, I don't know what the hell happened, I really don't. But now it's too late to do anything about it, because I'm already in love with her.

She moved in with us after she signed the blood oath. She shares my room. I guess it's our room now. The other girls don't know. I'm not ready for them to know. It would cause weirdness between all of us. Jealousy. Whatever. I'll tell them eventually. Just not now. Not yet. It's not that I'm ashamed of us or anything, it's just ... it's politics, you know? Even though we're a family and share everything, I want to keep this private. Just for now. Just until we're ready.

Z is amazing. Oh man, she's so, so, *so* great. I never really felt like anyone cared about me, you know? Not like she does. She makes me these special fancy meals. And cookies. Cookies! She rubs my feet, my back. She draws these crazy awesome portraits of me in her sketchbook. She ... she makes me feel beautiful.

It's like she can see through me. Can see right into my soul. I know that sounds cheesy as fuck, but I don't know how else to describe it. I can't fake anything with her, know what I mean? It's real. In one life, I'm this hard-ass gang-banger taking the world on, but when I'm alone with her, there's no more armour, there's no more walls, I'm just this sappy puddle of joy. It's terrible, I know. There are so many reasons I shouldn't be doing this. It can only end badly. It's not good. But right now, it's *so* good. I don't know what to do. I can't stop it; I tried and it didn't work. She's too good. She's gentle. She's kind. She's funny. She's smart. She's a brilliant artist. It's like she's everything I've always wanted to be but could never be. And she's put in mad work for the Black Roses. Not only does she bomb the city with our name and make it look wicked stylie, she's also taking care of all the little details: the groceries, the meals, the laundry, the bills. She cleans—she actually likes to clean. God, I don't know. It's stupid. It's too good to be true. It can't be real, and it can't last. All I know for sure is this: I love her like I've never loved anyone ever before. And when I look into her eyes, I see infinity.

I'd take a bullet for that girl, I really would.

KAYOS

It's really fucking annoying to have to stay home all week with your parents. I feel like I'm on house arrest. Yo, I actually went to school this week. Believe it. It was *so* weird. Seriously. I should probably start dealing at school since I'm gonna be there anyway. Lotsa preps at my high school are into coke now. All shiny and happy with their fucking argyle sweater vests. *God.*

My parents think I'm sick or something, otherwise I'd be out all the time like usual. Roger rented me a bunch of movies. Brought me some Gatorade. He hasn't touched me in a long time. Not since I threatened to tell my mom. I think it would destroy him to lose her. I wouldn't care about that so much, except that I know it would ruin her life. For real. As much as it's totally fucked up what he did, Mom wasn't doing so good before she met him. Okay, she was a mess. She's better now. She's off the booze. The Valium. Everything. She just shops and gets her hair and nails done, looks after Laura, and makes muffins and shit. I think she's happy. I don't know.

I saw some coverage about the shooting on the news. The reporter said the police think it's gang-related. Well, no shit. A known gangster gets gunned down in the street. Could it be gang-related? Ya think? Dumb pigs. His name was Christopher Johnston. He was from Surrey. Anyway, that seems to be about all they know, so I guess that's good, right? Oh yeah, and there was a number to call at the bottom of the screen if you have any information. Crime Stoppers or some shit. No reward or nothing. Nobody will call. I'm pretty sure of that. They better not. Or I'm fucked.

I've been waiting to feel bad about it. Guilty or depressed or haunted, whatever. I thought I would, but I don't. I don't feel anything. All I know is that I killed somebody. And if I had to, I could do it again.

When it came on the news, I was holding Laura on my lap, and I just squeezed her. I squeezed her so tight around the belly, without even realizing I was doing it, until she kind of gasped and squirmed away.

She's getting so big now. She's actually kind of fat. Ha ha. I like it, though; she's fat like a little healthy baby should be. She'll be three next fall. I can hardly believe I had her almost three years ago. It seems like a lifetime ago. I told Mom I'm gonna put Laura to bed tonight. I'll give her a bath first. Then read her a bedtime story. One of the ones I used to like. Maybe that one about the kid who flushes his mom's watch down the toilet, but she doesn't get mad because she'll love him forever.

I know Laura is his, and what we did was so wrong for so many reasons, but she's still my kid, right? I mean, I'm allowed to love her. I'm allowed that, at least.

PART 2
STREETS OF PLENTY

MERCY

Just as I expected, the shooting blew over in about a week. It was mentioned in the papers and on the news, but as far as we could tell, there wasn't much of an investigation happening. I mean, who really cares about some scumbag Slurrey gangster taking a fall anyway? And you know all the junkies on Hastings will keep quiet about whatever they saw. Even if there's a reward, they'll keep their mouths shut. Because if they snitch on us, they know they're a) going down and b) never going to be able to buy off us again. So you'd better believe they clam up. It's just the code of the streets. You don't snitch. What do the rappers say? Oh yeah, snitches get stitches. True enough.

When we were rolling with the Vipers, Mac put a hole through a guy's hand for snitching. Dumb fuck let it get infected, and eventually they had to cut off his whole arm. Now everybody calls him the one-armed rat.

Mac let Sly Girl take it easy the day after the shooting, and didn't ask her to go out on the corner or anything. I don't think Sly would have been able to anyway, she was pretty messed up. Quivering like one of those nervous little dogs and looking like hell. I guess she was sick or something, I don't know. It's not like she's never seen anything like that before, her life's been pretty rough from what she's told us, but I guess she was taking this kind of hard. But the next morning, Mac said Sly had to get back out there, because it would look suspicious if we were gone for too long. Plus, every day we don't sell drugs on East Hastings we lose about a thousand dollars.

You can go out in the afternoon, broad daylight, it's gonna be totally fine. Look, it's even sunny out. You wanna go with her, Mercy?

Nope.

Aw, come on.

Sorry, I'm busy. I've got a Benz, a Beemer, and a Hummer to find.

For fuck's sakes, Mac said under her breath. Fine. Fine. I'll go with her. Can you be ready in twenty minutes?

Sly Girl nodded.

Great. Mac motioned for me to follow her into her room and shut the door behind us. How's Kayos doing? she asked, as she got her gun out of her dresser drawer.

Fine, I think. I flopped down on her unmade bed.

Nothing about any of this gets said over the phones, right?

I rolled my eyes.

Right?

Come on, Mac! How long have we been doing this?

Alright, alright, just gotta make sure.

A little credit, please? You're talking to a professional here.

You're right, girl. You're right. I'm sorry. She put her hand around my shoulder and gave it a squeeze. Hey, you been stealing anything good lately?

Sure have.

Oh yeah? What?

I got an $1,800 Prada purse yesterday.

Really? Her eyes popped. Wow.

You can have it if you want, I shrugged.

Aw, shit, you know me. I ain't really the purse-carrying type. But hey, we should go shopping soon. I want to pick up some new clothes, maybe get some boots or something.

Yeah, sure. Whenever you want. I smiled at her.

And Z should come too. Girl wears the same damn clothes every day.

I sighed. I don't know, Mac. Three people draws more attention, you know?

Oh. Okay. I guess you're right. I'll just pick some stuff out for her, I guess.

I shrugged.

Hey, Mercy?

I looked up at Mac's reflection in the mirror where she was putting her eyeliner on, thick and black.

You're the best, she said.

No, you are.

You are!

Okay, you're right, I am. It was our old game. We'd say it out on the corner when we were working for the Vipers, trying not to feel insecure. Go back and forth, back and forth, until someone finally gave up and admitted to being the best.

I love Mac, you have to understand that. She's like the sister I never had. But something's changed in her since we started this thing of ours. She's all about the money and the power now. Well, maybe she always has been. I can't help but wonder how long it'll be until we can both get out of the game for good.

VANCOUVER

The morning glows around me, the concrete sucking up the light. But my concrete is beautiful, never more so than in the rain. At the birth of the new day, I am already heavier than the night before. Heavy with newness; three hundred steel cranes, freshly poured cement, slabs laid so thick they block out the sky, immaculate shimmering buildings, reaching, reaching, forever reaching up.

The bridge soaring over the silver bay is already clogged with the cars of workers. A million hard and lonely workers who want to vanish into me, want me to somehow fix them, want nothing more than to believe in the city of their dreams.

KAYOS

I miss my girls, yo. For real. No, you don't understand, I mean, I *really* miss them. Fuck! It's like I'm rotting away over here. Seriously. I have to get outta this house. I miss downtown, just being there, you know? Just being a part of it all. Believe it or not, I even miss some of our customers. Whacked, right? You know that junkie with the coat-hanger shoulders, wears that green and yellow tracksuit all the time? As fucked up as his life is, he always has a huge smile for everybody. Calls me Red. And Lacey, that crackhead who used to be a hairdresser? She always goes on about how nice my hair is, how she can't believe it's my natural colour, and how she'd kill to have colour like mine. Once, when she was coming up short, I let her give me a haircut in exchange for a rock. I needed a trim anyway. Yo, she did a better job than Magicuts! I don't know. It's weird. Yeah, they're all mangled, but they're people too, right? Some of them are pretty sweet.

Every time my phone rings, or I get a text, I think it's gonna be Mac telling me it's safe to come down again. But it never is.

I've been having weird dreams. A gun going off in my face. Walking around downtown but not being able to see where I'm going. These loud explosions all around me. My hands all covered in blood. Black blood.

When I think about shooting that guy now, I can't even believe that it happened. I can't believe it was me who did it. What the hell happened to me? I used to be a fucking Girl Guide, for chrissakes.

We need to get a safe, Mac sez 2 me 1 day outta da blue.

O ya?

Yeah. I mean, we can't really open bank accounts with all this cash, that would leave a paper trail, right? We can't keep buying furniture and art and shit, we gotta start saving for our condo.

R condO?

Yeah! A really gorgeous waterfront condo, baby. Get the fuck outta dodge, start living like the queens we are!

$he ki$$e$ me den & her lipz R tastee lyke da most delihu $hugar frootz in da wyde wurld. i grab her a$$ & we roll around on da bed 4 a-wyle, playin.

Whoz gonna live dere?

All of us, I guess.

1 big happee famlee, eh?

$he $hrugz. We're all working for it, Z.

i know, i know. ju$t … i want U all 2 myself sumtimes, U know?

She laffs, rolls her sexee green eyez. Maybe we can have a private suite or something, okay?

U sure U can buy a condO w/ ca$h?

$he give$ me di$ look.

Wat? im ju$t $ayin, mebbe deres sum law agnst it or $umpin …

Cash buys everything, baby. You know that.

aiight, $o … we'll get a $afe.

A big one.

ma$$ive.

Bolt it to the floor.

bolt U 2 da floor, c'mere grrl! i grab her & $tart tickling her, ki$$ing her evrywhere.

Shh! Stop it! Stop, Z. They'll hear us! Z…

i don't give a fuck.

$he ki$$es my lipz, $weetlee, tendrlee.

U ki$$ by da book.

evn tho i had left my famlee, wuz involved in cryme evry day, & dropped outta HI$kewl, i knew da Black Roses were da be$t thing 2 evr happen 2 me. Mac wuz da be$t thing 2 evr happen 2 me. i M po$itively $ure about dat.

SLY GIRL

Only time I feel halfway normal now is when I'm hittin the pipe. I know I shouldn't be. I know it's riskin everythin to smoke. But what choice do I have, really? My life has been too fucked up to live sober. Some days, I wake up, and I'm surprised, eh. I'm surprised I'm still alive, still here, you know?

But I got friends now at least. They're good to me. We're kinda like a little family, like a real family should be. Stickin together. Lookin out for each other. Better than the family I left behind.

Why?

Cuz I know these chicks aren't gonna kill me. If they find out I'm smokin crack, they'll kick me outta the house and outta the Black Roses, but that's the worst that's gonna happen. In my old house, there was always a chance you'd wake up dead, or worse.

Sometimes, when I'm lyin in bed at night, I think about my grandmother. Think about how she used to hold me on her lap and brush my hair with her special wooden comb. How she'd play cards with me and let me help her peel potatoes. I think maybe my grandmother is the only person who ever loved me. I'd like to see her again. Tell her I'm okay. Tell her I'm alive. Tell her I forgive her. That it wasn't her fault. But that would mean going back. And I can't ever go back.

KAYOS

The only time I feel halfway normal now is when I'm kicking the shit outta someone in kickboxing. Just givin er, letting everything come out. But last night, I got in shit with my Sensei because I went too hard on this dude I was sparring with and didn't stop kicking him when I should have. I don't even know what happened, yo. I kinda just blanked out for awhile. Anyway, turns out buddy's got three broken ribs because of me, so I feel pretty bad about that. Sensei said I gotta take it easy for a while, and I'm not allowed to come back to the gym for a couple weeks, not till I've cooled off. I apologized to the guy and everything, but Sensei was really upset. He said if it happens again, I'll be banned from the club.

Sometimes I feel like I'm losing it, I really do. I don't know what's wrong with me. Sometimes I wake up in the morning, and all I want to do is hurt people. That's gotta be fucked up.

MERCY

I love cars. Love driving them, stealing them, working on them, racing them, all of it. My dad taught me a lot about cars while he was around; maintenance and repair, how to change a tire, stuff like that. The Vipers taught me everything else I needed to know. Guess I can thank them for that, if nothing else.

I always thought my life would have been a whole hell of a lot easier if I'd been born a man. Then I could've been a pilot or a race-car driver or something legit, instead of just ripping people off for a living. Don't get me wrong, I love being female; wearing heels, dressing posh, jewellery, makeup, all that, but it just doesn't lead to the same opportunities, you know?

I guess I can tell you about what happened the other night. As long as you promise not to tell anyone. Ever. Swear on your life.

Okay. So, on this particular night I'm forgetting about all that I could have been and just living who I *am*, right there in the moment. I'm cruising in a silver Jaguar XK I picked up over in Yaletown, listening to Nas, bass cranked. The sky had just opened up and turned the city into an aquarium. But I'm all happy and dry inside my little silver bullet. I wish I didn't have to drop off the Jag, I wish it was mine for keeps. But, for the short distance to the Port of Vancouver, it is. I crank the heat and let it blast in my face. I'm noticing how smooth the road is under these tires, how soundless the car is; the streets are like black blankets laid out before me.

Then I'm on East Pender and out of nowhere, *bang!* A body

crumples under the hood. There's a sickening bump as my tires pass over it. *Oh-fuck-oh-fuck-oh-fuck-OH, FUCK!*

I check the rear-view. There's a guy lying in the middle of the road, his black raincoat billowing around him like a garbage bag. There's no one on the street. It's four in the morning. No one's around. Nobody saw it. I don't know what to do. I do not know what to do. I. Do. Not. Know. I keep driving.

Mac! Wake up! Someone was pounding on my door. *Mac!*

I rolled over, looked at Z. She was sound asleep. It was 4:20. The pounding got louder. I opened the drawer beside my bed and took out my gun, wiped the crusties out of my eyes, then got up and opened the door.

Mac—

What is it? What's wrong?

I hit someone.

What?

I just hit a guy crossing the road. With a car.

Oh Jesus. Where?

On East Pender.

Did anyone see you?

I don't know, no. No! She stared at the gun in my hand. She was shaking like she had hypothermia, her thin little face all crunched in panic.

I tossed the gun on my dresser. Alright, just try to calm down, I said. We'll deal with it. I walked past her and looked out the window. There was a silver Jag parked in our driveway. What the fuck is that doing here? Have you lost your mind? Get rid of that fucking car! Get it out of here!

I—I have to clean it first. There's some blood on the hood.

Well, go do it somewhere else. Get that car the fuck out of here right fucking now! You can't have that car anywhere near this place. Are you insane? Take it down the street, clean it off, and go drop it off at the port. I'll be waiting for you at the gates.

Here. I handed her a towel. *Go!*

Okay, okay. She hurried out the door.

Christ's balls, what was this, amateur hour? She must be in shock. I gathered a couple of old sheets, some garbage bags, and a cardboard box. I went back to my room and kissed Z on the cheek. I gotta go out for a bit, baby.

She moaned. Why? Where're you going?

I just gotta take care of something quick. I'll be back real soon.

She moaned again and rolled over.

I grabbed my gun and a hacksaw, then got into the Honda and drove the thirty seconds to meet Mercy in front of the entrance to the port.

She got in, her big deer eyes all glassy and wide.

You drop the car?

Yeah.

You didn't say anything to them, right?

No.

You get the blood off?

Yeah. But … there was a little dent.

Shit. Well, nothing we can do about that. Maybe they won't notice and think it happened in the shipping yard. Let's find your guy.

I drove over to Pender and saw a dark lump in the middle of the street. I pulled over and scanned the area, looking for any signs of activity. There was a little bit of movement in the alley to the west, but no one was on the sidewalk or the street. Except for the lump. It was crack hour; everyone was holed up with their pipes or sleeping off a heroin binge.

That where you left him?

She nodded.

No one has moved him? No one has touched him?

I don't think so.

A black Durango cruised by us. *Fuck!* But they didn't slow down. They probably thought the body was a garbage bag. That's what it looked like.

What should we do?

I think we should move it.

Why?

Why? So the cops don't come sniffing around trying to find out what happened. So there's no investigation, no tie-in to an illegal car-theft ring. This is serious, Mercy. If we get caught over this, and Lucifer's Choice gets busted, we'll all be killed.

I know! God! I'm sorry, Mac. I'm so sorry. It was an accident. I didn't mean to hit him! She began to cry.

I know you didn't. Let's just deal with it, okay? I grabbed the garbage bag and sheets and got out of the car. We gotta move fast.

We walked over to the body. He had a gnarly grey beard and a dirty face. He reeked of booze. He was probably homeless. His icy blue eyes stared up at us, and his mouth hung open, as if he was about to ask a question.

What are we going to do with him?

I laid the sheet down on the road. We're gonna hide him in plain sight. Here, help me roll him onto the sheet.

Once we had him cocooned in the sheet, we half-dragged,

half-heaved him up onto the sidewalk and into the entrance of the nearest alley. There were a couple people in it, further down, but they were wrapped in blankets, sleeping. Okay. I ripped the cardboard and put it down on the ground. Then we rolled him off the sheet and onto the cardboard. I covered him with a garbage bag as if it were a blanket and adjusted his arm, which was bent at a sickening angle.

Alright, let's get the fuck out of here, I whispered.

Wait. Mercy pulled her sleeve over her hand and knelt beside the man. She brushed her hand over his face and closed his eyes. Then she closed hers. She took a deep breath and let it out slow. Okay, she nodded once, and we walked back to the car with our heads bent to the rain.

We're not gonna mention anything about this to the others, I said as I started the ignition.

Okay. She stared down at her hands.

The less they know, the better.

She swallowed, nodded.

I don't trust them yet, I said. Do you?

No, but I will.

When we got home, we both had showers, then smoked a little joint. I left Mercy on the couch watching a mind-numbing nature documentary and went to bed. Z threw her arm across my belly and murmured something about chocolate milk. I lay awake for a long time, thinking, listening to the sounds outside, bottle-pickers' carts clattering in the back alley, junkies yelling, cars backfiring, dogs howling, rain falling, glass smashing, and the city tearing itself apart.

VANCOUVER

Not all cities are created equal.

MERCY

That was too fucked up.

Mac and I smoked a fat joint when we got home, but it did nothing to calm me down. I think I was in shock, I don't know. I stayed up for awhile watching TV, then went into my room as the sky started to lighten. I covered myself in blankets and lay in bed, shivering, seeing that man's cold blue eyes staring up at me. Everywhere I looked, all I could see were his eyes. Sad eyes, milky-blue.

I knew I probably wouldn't get caught, but in a weird way I sort of wanted to be. I'd killed a civilian. Someone who had nothing to do with the game was dead because of me. I was just as bad as those fuck-wads who did drive-bys and gunned down pregnant women and straight-A students who just happened to be in the wrong place at the wrong time. What about Blue Eyes' family? His friends? They would probably think he drank himself to death. They would never know the truth. No one would. The guilt pressed down on me like a car compactor. Even though it was an accident, I hated myself for what I'd done.

KAYOS

Finally, finally, *finally*, Mac said I could come downtown again. I was so relieved. I hopped on the next bus and rode it straight to the house on Cordova. It felt like it had been a hundred years since I'd been there, for real, but I guess it had really only been two weeks.

What's up, my bitches? I hugged them all super tight. And they hugged me right back.

Mercy had a joint all rolled up for me when I got there, and I told her I loved her.

So, how was your hiatus? Mac asked.

Pretty boring. I actually went to school, yo.

Oh yeah? Learn anything?

Yeah, I guess I did, I laughed. I learned that a lot of kids are doing coke now, and it would be a hot market to target. For real.

Your high school?

Yeah.

I don't think that's a good idea, Kayos.

Come on, it'd be so easy! Seriously. That shit practically sells itself.

No.

What? Why not?

Think about it.

Seems like a good idea to me. I shrugged and looked at Sly Girl and Mercy.

Well, it's not. It's a fucking stupid idea.

Why? I felt like she'd slapped me.

Mac looked at Mercy, then passed me the joint and exhaled a long, thin stream of smoke toward the ceiling. Really?

What? I thought we could get some new customers. Get a little more cash flow going on.

First of all, it's not a controlled environment. There's too many narcs in a school, not everyone does drugs, not everyone likes people who do drugs or sell them. And there's always some dumb-shit kid looking to be a hero by ratting out a dealer. Not to mention parents who like to get way too involved in their kids' lives. Second, we can make coke into crack and sell it for ten times as much, so it would be a waste of our time and money to sell just straight coke. And I'm sure as fuck not selling crack to high school kids. And third, we sell drugs in the Downtown Eastside because this is where the addicts live. There is no better market. They would be here with or without us. I don't feel too good about getting some promising junior varsity type hooked on blow, do you?

I guess not.

Please think it all the way through next time you come up with a good idea. I can't be the only one using my brain around here. She went into the kitchen. We heard dishes clattering in the sink.

I missed you too! I yelled. Damn, who pissed in her cornflakes?

Don't worry about her. She's been under a lot of stress lately, Mercy said.

Yeah? Well, so have I.

We sat in silence for a while and finished the joint. Sly Girl began rolling another one.

What's been going on around here, anyway?

Well, said Mercy, Z got arrested last night.

i wuz in da middle of doin di$ kiLLR piece ovR in $tanlee prk, on da $eawall, aiight? $ed BlAcK RoSes in wyld $tyle w/ ro$es & thornz rapt around da lettrz. it wuz $ick. Mac came w/ me, ju$t 2 keep me cumpanee & 2 watch, but $he'd gone 2 buy u$ $um $mokes, next thing i know, da red & bluez R fla$hin in my face, on da megafOne, tellin me get my damn handz UP. i'm lyke, fuck thi$, & take off. didn't get 2 far tho, $toopid $hort legz. next thing i know i'm on my bellee w/ cop kneez in my bak, gettin cuffed & $huved in da cruzr. well, i'm pi$$ed cuz i didn't get 2 fini$h da piece, & U no an unfini$hed piece is a $erious failure, a totL $tryke against U. but itz a tynee bit Xciting becuz i've nevR bin aRRe$ted b4. az we're pullin out, i C Mac cumN bak w/ 2 lrg coffeez 4 u$. $he eyez UP da cruzr, but of cour$e itz dark $o $he can't C me in$yde. i want 2 mah da windO & jump out 2 her. i bang my hed again$t da gla$$ becuz i want her 2 know i'm in here. but nuthin happenz xcept my hed getz $ore & da cop in da pa$$enger $eat turnz round & glarez @ me & tellz me 2 take it EZ lyke i'm $um nutjob. Mac keepz walkin & doe$n't look @ da car again. But i know $he'll figger it out when $he C's my sprAy canz all ovR da ground & da unfini$hed werk.

$o dey take me downtown & fingRprint me & take my foto & tell me i'm in a holelottashit. Tell me i'm bein charged w/ MI$CHIEF under section 430(1) under da criminal code of canada. tell me i'll be doin communitee service til i'm 65 cuz dey know i'm da 1 whoze bin wrytin BlAcK Roe all ovr de

Ntyre goddamned citee & dey've $pent about a million doll-hair$ cleenin it up alreadee. hee hee hee, oop$! & den dey tell me i get 1 fone call & it bettr B 2 some1 whoza Leegul Gardeean & can promise dat i'll keep my court appointmentz, coun$elling appointmentz & communitee $ervis appointmentz. dey tell me dat i'm gonna be on Hou$e Arre$t & i'm gonna wi$h i'd never picked up a $prAy can. ya, ryte.

of cour$e i'm lyke, oh fuck my lyfe, Bcuz da onlee person i want 2 call iz Mac but $he iz not my Leegul Gardeean & $he's not evn 18 yet so wat da fuck M i poed 2 do? i havn't $poken 2 my parentz in about 3 monthz, but if i don't call dem i'll haf 2 $pend da night in jayle!!!!

$o i call dem.

VANCOUVER

They give me small gifts, the people of my city, visitors too; shapes, letters, murals, tiles, posters. Images they find beautiful or ugly, shocking or amusing, they plaster to my surfaces. Words they deem important they carve into me. Now a bronze sculpture, now a giant knitted cap, now a pair of running shoes dangling from a wire. I accept each of these gifts with endless gratitude, knowing that the person who made it has shaped me, just as I have shaped them. We are bound forever. They will take what they have gleaned from me wherever they go; Toronto, L.A., New York. I imagine them there, whispering into the fog, *I love Vancouver.*

MAC

I can't believe Z got caught. After two years of writing and never getting taken down, the one night I go with her, *the one night*—boom. I must be her bad luck charm. And now her parents got her on lockdown or some shit and she can't even leave the house. It's insane. I gotta go bust her out in a day or so if she can't get away from them. They're crazy, man. I'm talking *in*sane.

They forced her to play piano when she was a little girl. She told me they would make her play piano for two hours every day no matter what. She wasn't allowed to get up off her piano bench until she sat there for two hours. One day she pissed her pants because they told her she wasn't finished practising yet. Here she is, twelve years old, with pee running down her pant legs and dripping onto the foot pedals.

I've gotta get her out of that nuthouse. They took away her cell phone so I can't even call her. I tried the number at her parents' but someone just picked up, listened for a minute, and hung up again. Maybe one of her sisters. Apparently they're psycho-bitches. Well, I'll come up with some way to get her out. She can't keep living there, that's for sure.

The good news is we have nearly three hundred grand in cash right now. The bad news is I still haven't gotten a safe. I've gotta go out today and get one. For sure. I've been stashing it all up in a ceiling tile, but I don't feel too good about that. Not with this amount of cash.

But pretty soon, we're gonna be able to move out of here.

We're gonna actually be able to own our own place, a real sweet-ass place. I can't risk that not happening. I wish I could just put it all in the bank like a normal person, but what am I gonna say? Oh yeah, hi, I made this money at my job ... flipping burgers. Right. I thought about saying it was an inheritance or something, but I don't know. I wouldn't want anyone to get suspicious, you know? Anyways, my Uncle Hank knows a guy in real estate who'll set us up, no problem. I'll just give him a call when the time gets closer.

SLY GIRL

I know I'm not sposed to front nobody, but today Cindy comes up to me all strung out, and she's got her head shaved and it looks real awful, it's a real messy shave. I know I'm no one to be sayin anythin about other people's looks, but damn. I mean she looks like she's about to go in for brain surgery or somethin, eh, and she's all, please, please, please, Rachel-ing me. She knows my real name cuz we knew each other from before, when I was livin out here. We worked the same spots, got high together, and everythin. She'd helped me out once with a bad date, probably saved my life. Anyways, I'm like, What's with your haircut?

I don't know! She's all shifty-eyed, lookin around everywhere.

What do you mean, you don't know?

I mean, I don't fuckin know! Not a fuckin clue. I woke up this morning and it was like this. Freaked me right out, man. Someone came by and did it to me in the night.

That's fucked up.

You're telling me!

And you have no idea who it was?

She shrugged three times. Don't know. Don't know. So, whaddya say, honey? Do me a favour today, hon? I can pay you tomorrow, I promise. I swear to God. I just haven't worked yet today, you know, so … well, you know how it is! She scratched her stubbly head. Her hair had been shoulder-length, wavy, oil-slick black. She actually had real nice hair. *Please, Rachel?* With a cherry on top? I swear I'm good for it. Cross my heart, hope to die. She crossed an X over her heart with her cigarette-stained fingers. You know I'm good for it!

Yeaah, I know. Hold on a sec, k? I'll check. I walked around the corner to where Mac was waitin for me, blowin smoke rings up to the skyscrapers. Mac, I know you said I can't never give credit, but I need to front Cindy today.

Her face went all serious and she smushed her cigarette into the sidewalk. Come on, Sly Girl—

Someone shaved off all her hair last night while she was sleepin.

Jesus. Fuckin weirdo junkies. She spit into the gutter. What does she want?

Just a couple ten rocks.

She good for it?

Yeaah.

No, she's not, Sly. She's a crack whore, alright? She's good for nothing.

It's just that she's kind of—

What?

She's sorta ... well, she's kinda a friend of mine. From before.

Mac sighed. Shook her head. Alright, just this once. Not again, okay? Not for her, not for anybody. She can't ask again. Tell her that. And if she doesn't pay, she's gonna get a lot worse than a shaved head. Tell her that too.

Okay. Thanks, Mac. As I watched Cindy hurry away, her bony shoulder blades poking out the back of her hoodie, I felt a fierce sadness rush into me. I'm not sure why, exactly. Maybe because I knew that, in a lot of ways, me and her are the same.

my parentz rnt lettin me outta my room til i'm 30. dey took my fone! O GOD i mi$$ Mac $o BAD. Aaaahhhhh! im goin NUTZ!!! i havnt been out $ince i got picked up. my parentz R craZee, man. dey watchin me 24/7. think ima run away again which i M Bcuz di$ aint no kinda lyfe 4 Z up in here. cant do my aRt cant luv my luvr WTF!!???!!! dey $et an alarm @ nite so if i open a wyndO or door it goe$ off. how da FUCK M i gonna get outta here?

my $i$terz R fuckin a$$holes, man. dere all lyke, Where have you been, little missy? Getting high? Got a boyfriend now? Who's your boyfriend? What have you been doing? Hey? Hey? Dey poke me in da ribz, in da belly. tell me ima fat whore.

im lyke, $hut up U uglee bitchez. get back in yr ba$ement $uite. mind yr own.

1 $tudeez law & 1 iza web dvlpr. dey R twinz. i h8 dem both & dey have alwayz h8d me. dey tell me i wuz an aXident. dat i nevr $huda been born. da grrlz in da Black Roses R more $i$terly 2 me den my own $i$terz have evr been.

my parentz R gonna put me in coun$elling. i hafta do communitee $ervi$. pickin up $yringez & $hit off da street. $ICK!!! i'm gonna get AIDS!!! i gotta go 2 de$e weekly $e$huns da pigz put on about how vandalyzm hurtz evry1. im not poed 2 have contact w/ NE of my crew & i gotta go back 2 HI$kewl. fuck it, my lyfe iz ovr.

KAYOS

I really can't stand going to high school for one more day. I mean, I know I'm smart. I don't need some piece-of-shit diploma to tell me that. I can't take it anymore. I just can't. It's all preps and jocks and nerds. There's no one like me. Everyone fucking sucks in that school, I swear to God. They think they're so important, that their lives are so dramatic, so interesting. God, spare me. Yo, I almost puked yesterday when I overheard these chicks in the bathroom talking about who they were going to the dance with and what they were gonna wear. I mean, this is their life: boys, clothes, makeup, and gossip. They're like straight outta *Seventeen Magazine* or some shit. Seriously. How can I possibly relate to that? I spend most of my time in the DTES selling drugs to strung-out junkies. When I'm not doing that, I'm pulling ATM scams or boosting. When I'm at home, I'm looking after my two-year-old kid and trying to avoid Roger. I don't belong in high school. I'm not going anymore. What's the point?

MERCY

This weekend I boosted around fifteen grand worth of merchandise. I have to admit, it did make me feel a little better. I got a ton of sick outfits for all the girls: shoes, boots, handbags, jackets, makeup. Not because we need any of that shit, but because every now and then it's nice to get dressed up. Feel a little bit special. I got books, magazines, iPods, CDs, DVDs. I got two digital cameras, a butterfly knife, a Swiss Army watch, a Swarovski crystal bracelet, silver bangles, gold hoop earrings—so much jewellery I could open a kiosk.

I'm not sure if we're going to keep it all or pawn some of it or what. We haven't decided yet. I think we should keep it, because for some reason, having nice stuff makes you feel better about yourself. I don't know why. It just does.

When I got home, I dumped it all in the middle of the floor. Kayos, Mac, and Sly Girl were sitting in the living room taking hits from the bong and watching *Kids*. Their eyes bugged out of their heads when they saw the huge pile of stuff. It was precious.

Have at er, ladies. I stood back, grinning at the looks on their faces.

They began picking through the clothes, trying things on, laughing. Soon we were all wearing awesome outfits, crowded into the bathroom, doing our makeup in the mirror.

When's Z coming home? I asked Mac.

She sighed. I don't know. Her parents have her on lockdown. I'm afraid they're gonna ship her off to China to live with her grandparents or something.

We should go get her back. I mean, she belongs here with us, right?

Yeah! Kayos said, as she applied her new black liquid eyeliner. Let's go get that little juvenile delinquent!

Yeah? Mac said.

Yeah! All of us yelled.

Alright, she said, zipping up her new knee-length leather coat. Let's go.

MAC

Mercy came home with this mad shitload of stuff for us. Heaps of designer clothes, tons of makeup, and a bunch of jewellery. It's hard to believe she's never been caught stealing. The shit she gets away with, man, it's unbelievable. It's like she's the incredible invisible brown girl. She just walks into a place and takes whatever she wants and no one bats a fuckin eyelash. They should name a superhero after her.

I think we should try to resell most of it—either pawn it or just get rid of it on the street. I mean, it's nice stuff and everything, but we don't really *need* any of it. We need a condo in West Vancouver a lot more than we need skinny jeans. And we're getting real close to having enough for a down payment. But I have to admit, some of the stuff Mercy scored is pretty fuckin fly. I found a long, black leather coat in the pile of clothes. It had a nice soft finish. I picked it up and smelled the leather to make sure it was real and not that plastic shit.

It was real.

The lining was gorgeous—silk, dark red. Kayos and Sly Girl were already knee-deep in the pile of clothes, squealing like little girls. I slipped the coat on and adjusted the collar so it lay flat.

Mercy stared at me and grinned. I got that for you, Mac. Fits perfect.

No you didn't.

Oh yes, I did.

I looked at myself in the mirror. It did look great. It was the coat I had always wanted. It came to just below my knee and fit snug. I looked at the price tag. $2,850. Really? You got this for me?

Come on, don't get all emotional on me. It's not like I paid for it. She laughed.

Damn, girl. You look fiiiiine, Kayos said.

Yeah, Mac, you look hot. Sly Girl giggled in her nervous way, which I sometimes found annoying, but not right then.

Thanks.

Show us the back, yo.

I did a little twirl.

Ooohhhh!

Still want to sell all this down on the corner? Mercy asked, raising an eyebrow.

Okay, okay. I'll keep it, I laughed, and went back to the mountain of clothes in the middle of the room. The next thing I pulled out was a short, black bomber jacket, with a thousand zippered pockets, inside and out. Oh, this would be perfect for Z, I said.

Where's Z at? Kayos asked.

She's still on house arrest at her parents'.

How's she doing? Have you heard from her?

Nope. Her parents took away her phone. Fuckers.

When is she coming home? Mercy asked.

I don't know. Her parents have her on a tight leash. I'm scared they're gonna send her away to boarding school in China or some shit.

Let's go get her, Mercy said. She should be here with us, not rotting away in the basement of her parents' house, right?

I looked at her. I didn't think that Mercy really liked Z. I got the feeling she didn't care when Z got arrested, that she was jealous of our relationship, even though she didn't know all the details of it. She knew that Z and I had become very close; she probably thought that Z had taken over her position as my best friend, but it wasn't like that.

Yeah? I said, still staring at Mercy.

Yeah! Kayos yelled. Let's go get that little young offender! She smacked her newly painted lips together, then kissed the mirror, leaving raspberry-coloured lip prints in the centre.

Mercy nodded, still looking at me. And at that moment, something unspoken passed between us. With that nod, I realized that Mercy knew exactly what was going on between me and Z, and that it was okay, she understood, and that she was still my best friend, and always would be.

Okay then, I said, zipping up my new coat. Let's roll.

We all piled into the Civic and Mercy drove us over to Chinatown. I was so excited to see Z, my fingers trembled as I lit my cigarette. Butterflies dive-bombed in my belly at the thought of seeing her, holding her, kissing her. Even though it had only been a week, I missed her like mad. I hadn't been able to sleep, and had hardly eaten since the night she was arrested. I blamed myself for her arrest. If only I hadn't left her to get smokes, I could have been her lookout and seen the cops coming before it was too late.

Okay, what's the plan? Kayos asked.

Plan?

What? We're just gonna knock on the door and say, Yo, can Z come out and play?

Mercy said, How about: Hi, we're here to take your daughter away to help us with our criminal enterprise.

Sly Girl giggled from the back seat.

Okay, you're right. We need a plan. I rolled down the window, blew smoke into the wet night. Alright, how bout this? Kayos, you knock on the door, when they answer say you're selling something—

What am I selling?

Magazine subscriptions, chocolate, I don't give a fuck, just something to distract them, okay?

Can I sell Girl Guide cookies?

No!

Why not? She pouted. I've done that before. I know what to say.

Because you're too old to be a fuckin Girl Guide anymore, okay?

I could be a Pathfinder, she mumbled.

What the hell is a Pathfinder?

Pathfinders are what come after Girl Guides. You can be fourteen or fifteen, I think, and you still have to sell the cookies.

Okay, fine. You're a Pathfinder.

Cool.

So, you knock on the door, and try to sell them your cookies.

But I don't have any cookies.

Just tell them you're taking orders so you know how many you'll need when your group gets their shipment.

Okay.

Try to chat them up, talk about the weather, ask them where they're from and shit.

Yo, what if they don't speak English?

Improvise!

Okay!

Mercy and I will go around to the back door and get Z out. Sly Girl, you stay in the car, watch the front door. Make sure everything's cool. If one of her parents leaves the doorway, start honking the horn, create a distraction. Got it?

Uh-huh.

Kayos, you'll just wrap it up and walk away when you see the car leave. We'll pick you up down the street at the four-way.

Got it.

Okay, that's the house. Park down the street a little ways, Merce.

After Mercy shut off the ignition, I surveyed them all. Okay, ready?

Born ready, baby.

Yep.

Mmhmm.

Let's go. I stepped out of the car and crushed my cigarette into the pavement with the heel of my boot. I was going to get my girlfriend back.

mom & dad were watchin tv out front & i wuz drawing in my room when i heard da doorbell. my heart seezed up 4 a sekond & i got di$ quihy feelin in my gutz. i can't xplain it, i ju$t knew it wud be her. i opened my door a crak so i cood li$ten. i wuz pretty $ure it wuz Kayo$ @ da door tryin 2 con my parentz in2 buyin cookeez or $um $hit. i laffed & opened my wyndO, $tuck my hed out. Mercy & Mac were dere $tarin up @ me. i $myled $o big my face hurt.

Come on, girl! What are you waiting for? Mac haf whi$pered haf yelled up 2 me. i wuz $o happee 2 C her i coodn't think $trayte. i ju$t $tood dere $tarin @ her. Come on!

i grabbed my wallet & tipeetoed down$tair$. my heart wuz a jackhammer in my chest, i wuz $o $cared my parentz wud C me or $top me or $omethin. but i managed 2 get 2 da bak door in da kitchen w/out dem $eein me. i cood heer Kayo$ chatterin away 2 dem. just az i $lid da gla$$ door open i herd my mom call my name, i was outta dere. a car alarm $tarted going off az $oon az i got out$ide. Mac grabbed my hand & we ran & ran & ran. i didn't know where we were going & it wuz dark but i wuz w/ Mac $o i knew evrything wud B OK. i ran az fast az i cood. we got 2 da car & Mercy $tarted er up & we were gone. $ly Girl wuz $ittin $hotgun & Mac & i were in da bak.

AHhHahaha! i yelled. wat took U bitchez so long?

dey all laffed az we $ped down my $treet. wen Mercy turned on 2 Keefer & pulled up 2 da curb, i reached 4 Mac & ki$$ed her on da lipz. i coodn't help it. it had been 2 long & i had mi$$ed her SO much. i didn't care who $aw or who knew. fuck it. i loved her & i needed her right then & 4 alwayz. $he ki$$ed me back & it wa$ lyke a million fyrewerx goin off in da bak seat of dat little honda. i nevr wanted 2 $top. dere wuz $ilence up front. Mercy cleered her throat & turned on da radio. no1 $ed a werd until Kayo$ got in da car a couple $econdz later, all giddy.

Yeah, bitches! $he $lapped u$ all hi-5. Alright, got our lil' Z back. Let's get the fuck outta here.

Mercy started the car. Where we going?

Mac gazed @ me, her eyez all mi$ty-luvey-dovey, Where do you want to go, Z?

let's go 2 a muvee.

A movie?

ya! we can go 2 tinseltown. get popcorn. make out. i whispered dat la$t part. it'll be gr8, i sed, tickling her thigh.

Mac grinned. Sound good?

evry1 agreed.

Alright, let's go see a movie.

i figured da muvee theatre wud be a fairlee $afe place. my parentz wudn't cum lookin dere & neether wud da copz. hell, we cood C 2 in a row. it didn't matter. all dat mattered wuz dat i wuz w/ Mac & i wuz free. & i knew 1 thing 4$ho, i wuz never goin hOme again.

MERCY

It was very fucking awkward to look in the rear-view mirror and see Mac and Z playing tonsil hockey in the backseat. I guess I should've seen it coming. I mean, they share a bed, for fuck's sake. But I had no idea. No fucking idea. In a way, I felt betrayed. I don't know why, it's not like I wanted to get with Mac or anything, but she was my best friend, I thought I knew her better than anyone, and I never knew she was into chicks. She'd always had boyfriends before. Lots of boyfriends. She never talked about girls that way. Never. She never once let on that she was ... you know. Like that.

I looked at Sly Girl and she laughed into her hand. I glanced at the back seat; they were still going at it. I cranked the radio, hit seek. I didn't feel right. This was weird. It was like suddenly I had no idea who Mac was. How long had they been hiding this from us? It's pretty fucked up when you think about it, actually.

Finally, Kayos got in the car and they stopped making out.

I drove fast, my mind numb, and no one said anything for awhile. Then, at an intersection, Kayos muttered, I can't get away from him.

What are you talking about? I said.

She pointed to a bench at the bus stop. It was plastered with the face of some moustache-wearing dumb-ass I'd seen before on billboards and shit. *Roger Jones Sells Homes!* it declared in big blue letters. That's my stepdad, she said.

I laughed. Your stepdad is Roger Jones?

Yeah.

Looks like a real douche.

He is.

Want me to paint over all his ads? Z piped up from the back.

I think you're taking a break from the paint for a while, baby, Mac said.

Z gave her a pouty mouth and their heads came together. I tried to keep my eyes on the road. Un-fuckin-believable, I whispered.

Sly Girl giggled, and I tilted the rear-view to check Kayos's reaction. Her mouth hung open and she stared without shame at the love scene going on beside her in the back seat.

We went to see a cheesy comedy at Tinseltown because that's what Miss Z wanted to do. I sat as far away from Mac as I could. I couldn't even look at her. I felt sick inside. I don't have a problem with gay people, I don't. But I *do* have a problem with my best friend hiding the fact that she's in a relationship with another friend of mine, who happens to be the same sex as her.

I couldn't even concentrate on the movie. All these thoughts were jamming up my head. I didn't even know if I could trust Mac again after this.

Later that night, after everyone had gone to bed, I took my .32 and balaclava and went out and robbed the twenty-four-hour liquor store at Cardero and Davie. This faggy little hipster was working the till. He didn't even flinch. Just flipped his hair back and handed over the cash like he'd done it a hundred times before. I got nearly eight hundred bucks.

SLY GIRL

After we broke Z out, we all went to Tinseltown to see *Resident Evil: Afterlife*. But they wouldn't let me in cuz it's rated R, and I look too young. Everyone was probably super pissed, cuz we all really wanted to see it, and the other movies looked lame. I thought the girls would probably go into *Resident Evil: Afterlife* anyways and leave me to watch a PG one on my own. But they didn't. They got their tickets changed so we could all see the same movie. That made me so happy, even though it was a stupid kids' movie, and I can't even remember the name of it. But at least we all got to sit together.

It's kinda funny actually, cuz here I am, already livin on my own two years now, workin the streets, sellin crack, makin crack, smokin, drinkin, and everythin else, you know, all these kinda adult things that kids don't do, or aren't sposed to do, but I still can't get into an R-rated movie. You gotta laugh at that.

When we got home, Mac and Z went into their room and closed the door, and Mercy went into her room and slammed the door. Or maybe it was the wind. Me and Kayos stayed up and smoked a joint.

Were you really a Girl Guide? I asked her.

Yeah, she laughed, and a puff of smoke came out her nose and made a little cloud around her head.

What kinda stuff did you have to do?

Dumb shit. Tie knots and sew buttons onto shirts, learn how to tell if a dog is sick. I just sold cookies mostly, except my mom would always have to buy them because I'd end up eating them all before I made any sales.

How can you tell if a dog is sick?

Its nose is dry.

Oh yeaah. I knew that.

I could go for some of those cookies right now, for real. She went into the kitchen, and I could hear her rootin around in the cupboards. She came back with a box of chocolate chip cookies and sat beside me on the couch. Dig in, yo.

I'd like to have a dog.

Seriously? You know you have to pick up their shit, right? she said, with her mouth full of cookie.

I shrugged. But don't you think it would be nice?

What, to pick up shit?

No! I laughed. To have someone who loved you no matter what. No matter what you looked like. No matter what you did or said, they would always love you the best. For as long as they lived.

Yeah, you're right. Dogs are cool.

We heard a low moan coming from Mac and Z's room, and we both stared at their door for a second.

Yo, what the hell is up with those two? Kayos whispered.

I shrugged. I dunno. I think they're in love or somethin.

Wow. Am I the only one who didn't know about that?

I shrugged again.

Dude, try to keep me in the loop, will ya?

Okay.

Okay?

Yeaah.

Yeah?

I laughed, and she hit me lightly in the shoulder.

Want to roll us up another j?

Uh-huh.

KAYOS

I curled up on the couch and laughed to myself. So Mac and Z were dyking out. Aw, it was funny, if nothing else. They'd hid it well. I didn't see that one coming *at all*. Seriously? Lesbo-G's? Not that I cared, I didn't. I just didn't want there to be shit going on that I didn't know about. I adjusted the sweater I was using as a pillow. At home in Shaughnessy, I had a queen-sized bed in a room of my own with an en-suite bathroom, but most nights I stayed here at the gang house, scrunched up in a corner of the stained, brown, L-shaped couch.

My mom didn't understand why I always wanted to sleep over at my friends' houses but never invited anyone to sleep over at our house. But she didn't know. She didn't know that when I was at home, all I felt like doing was hurting other people. Or myself. Sometimes, I even wanted to hurt her.

Why?

For being in denial. For not doing anything. For not realizing what was going on in her own house. Right under her nose in her own fucking home.

I wonder if I'll ever tell her the truth. So much time has passed now.

I'm still having these nightmares. Sometimes I wake up screaming. It's a real fucked-up feeling. The only place I can feel relaxed and safe, strange as it sounds, is here, on this couch, in this house, with these girls. So I sleep here most nights, and my dreams aren't so bad.

MERCY

Outside it's raining like it's never gonna stop. Me, Mac, and Kayos are sprawled around the living room. We've just had a long bong session and are sky-high.

Do you ever think of what you would do? Kayos asked. I mean, if you could do anything? If we didn't do this?

What do you mean? Mac snickered, and lit a cigarette. We're living the dream.

Yeah, Kayos laughed.

I sometimes think about being a clothing designer, I said. I would have my own clothing line with super sweet stuff. Like modern urban kinda gothic shit. But classic, too. And it would be comfortable but still super stylish. Everyone would buy it and want to come to my fashion shows. I'd have runway shows in New York, Paris, Tokyo. All the stars would wear my stuff to their premieres. And I would design wicked purses that didn't have straps that cut into your shoulder or bang against your leg. Purses you could always find your keys in.

Mac laughed. What would it be called?

My clothing line?

Yeah.

Queen Mab Designs.

Queen Mab?

She's like an evil fairy from dreamland ...

Jewellery too? Kayos asked.

Fuckin rights, the craziest most awesome jewellery you've ever laid eyes on!

And hair accessories?

Sure. Why not? And Queen Mab would make me so rich that I would be able to have a whole collection of cars. I'd have, like, twelve different cars that I got to drive around. A Lambo, a Porsche, a Rolls, a Jag, a hot pink Hummer, a Lotus—

So, Kayos said, what's stopping you from doing that right now?

Well, I kinda got this gang thing going on ...

They laughed, and I did too. But somehow, it wasn't funny. I lit a cigarette and thought about what other cars would be in my private collection.

Kayos and Mac started watching a movie, and I fell asleep on the couch. I dreamed about the guy in the street I had hit. He was yelling at me, but no sound was coming out of his mouth. I tried to hear him, I tried to read his lips, I tried so hard to understand. He kept coming closer and closer to me, till all I could see were his ice-blue eyes, the blood vessels in them all red and about to burst cuz he's so angry, yelling so hard in my face, but I can't hear.

I'm sorry! I say to him, I'm so, so, sorry. Then I wake up, and my eyes are all wet and I'm shaky. And it was a dream, but it was real, and that man is dead for real, and I killed him. I did to him what that driver did to my mom, and nothing can ever, ever, undo it.

VANCOUVER

A hard rain pours into me. Garbage is stacked head-high on the sidewalks, spilling onto the roads; the workers on strike, again. Loose debris and filth float through the streets, infecting gutters, ditches, and storm drains with an acidic stench. Later, as the indigo evening envelops the city, the sky finds total release, and all the scum is washed off the streets. Thousands of intersections turn silver in the rain. I watch over all the meetings, accidental and planned, at these glimmering crossroads. Some of them change lives forever.

SLY GIRL

I stayed home all day Saturday and made crack on the stove cuz Mac asked me to. The other girls had all gone out to work. It was pissin rain, so I didn't really want to go out anyways. I had the house to myself, so I had a few hits. I was doin pretty good with not smokin it all the time, though. I mean, I only had it once in a while now, not every day, twelve, fifteen times a day like before, when I was livin on the street. And I hadn't touched H since detox. I was doin okay.

Mac called around six, askin if I was hungry, said she was gonna meet up with the others at an Italian restaurant on Commercial, but I didn't feel like goin. Didn't feel like bein around all those beautiful hipsters and uptown mods, havin them all stare at my dog-food face. Especially since I was high.

Are you sure? Mac said. We can come pick you up.

Yeaah, no, I'm fine. I'll just order a pizza or somethin.

Okay, well, we'll see you when we get home then.

See you later, alligator. After I bagged up all the fresh, new, milky-white rocks, I decided to go down to Crack Alley for a bit and make some money. I knew the other girls had been out doin dirt all day with the ATMs, boosting and car stuff. I knew they would all be comin home with wads of cash, eh. And I wanted to, too.

I knew I wasn't really sposed to go out alone at night, but what the fuck? I'd lived out there for half a year on my own, hadn't I? I knew how to handle myself out there. I remembered to take my phone so I could call for backup if I needed to. I also got my .22 out of the closet and shoved it in my jacket pocket. I'd never fired it, but I liked to have it on me just in case, cuz you never know who you're gonna run into down there.

VANCOUVER

In an alley in the East End, there is a muffled scream that no one cares to hear. It bounces against the buildings and then is lost to the night. Then there is the silvery flash of a blade. There are thuds of skull hitting pavement, boots to bones, and flesh pounding into flesh.

The girl on the ground behind the dumpster came from elsewhere; she's the one with the crinkly eye. She keeps her eyes closed, doesn't move, while two men—boys, really—take from her everything they can. Her wrist is broken, her nose is broken, her rib is broken, she bleeds. She bleeds. The soft grey rain falls around her.

Her blood mixes with the rainwater and runs in dark rivulets into the low places in the alley; it pools with the urine and vomit of others who were here before. The boys cackle and slap each other's hands as they zip up their pants and sprint down the alley, their boots clicking over the pavement.

I love eating out at fancy restaurants, man. I don't know why, I always have. It just makes me feel normal for awhile, I guess. You know what I mean?

No?

Well, it's like, if you're out at a restaurant, being waited on, ordering food, ordering drinks, looking around at the other customers, you're inside, out of the rain. How bad can it be? Anyone eating at a restaurant has it pretty good, if you ask me. It means you're not dirt poor. It means you like yourself enough to treat yourself. And if you're not alone, well, that means somebody else likes you enough to share a meal with you.

So anyways, me, Z, Mercy, and Kayos went for dinner at this upscale Italian place on Commercial Drive called Lucia's. We'd had a good day; we wanted to splurge a little. Before I'd even ordered, I could feel people from other tables staring at me, at us. I saw some people whispering. Some greasy guys at the bar turned to look at us—Mafia guys, maybe. Yeah, yeah, I know what you're thinking. Paranoid, right? But just because you're paranoid doesn't mean people aren't out to get you. There's only so much to go around in this town, know what I mean?

I should've expected this. I don't know. I guess I thought we'd be more low profile than we are. But now I realize that was stupid. Look at us, G'd up from the feet up; all dressed in black, flashing bling, all packing. Yep, just four regular girls out to enjoy some spaghetti and meatballs! Is that normal? I hardly know anymore. I guess I'm just glad I prefer Italian food to Vietnamese. There's no way we could go in there. They know who we are, and they want us gone. I've seen where they've crossed out our name on the walls, written their own above. I've seen their girls in purple, glaring at us on the street. I just duck my head and keep walking. Avoid eye contact. Pretend like I'm no one. I don't need to start a beef with anyone, man. That's not what I'm about. I don't think that Black Roses' ad campaign was the smartest idea, now everyone knows who we are. I know that was the point, but it's not the way it should've been done. I see that now.

As our waitress set my plate in front of me, my phone buzzed. I checked the text. It was from Sly Girl. Her message said: 911 crak ally. I looked at my spaghetti, steaming red and smelling so good. I looked at the others, happily digging into their food. I threw two bills on the table and stood up. We gotta go.

VANCOUVER

Lights flicker around the girl's head; headlights bouncing off the wet pavement. She does not open her eyes. She lies perfectly still for a very long time. Later she stirs, reaches into her pocket, presses buttons. She touches the rose tattoo on her arm and waits.

Then they come for her. Her friends, the other four, come, and they wrap her in a blanket and heave her into the back of their tiny car. The spot where she fell glows red in the darkness of the alley.

MERCY

What the fuck happened to you? What the fuck happened to her?
Kayos is screaming in Sly Girl's face, then in my face, then
in Mac's. She is flipping the fuck out. I'm trying to drive but
keep looking in the rear-view at Sly Girl. She is bleeding, her
face is all puffy, and her bottom lip is the size of a donut. She's
stretched out across Kayos's lap. Kayos is holding her hand
and smoothing her hair away from her face. There is blood
in her hair, and Kayos wipes her hand on her new pants. Sly
Girl looks like she is pretty goddamn close to dying, but she
doesn't want to go to a hospital. We know because she said
no hospital. That's about the only thing she's said. I park in
front of our house, and we all carry her inside. Put her on the
couch, cover her in blankets. I bring her a bag of frozen peas
for her face. Kayos brings her a shot of Jack Daniel's and a tea.
Mac sits down beside her on the couch and tries to clean her
face with a wet washcloth.

Who did this to you?

Sly takes short, shallow breaths. You can tell she is trying
really hard not to cry.

These two crackheads ... jumped me in the alley ... took
everything ... all the rock, the cash, then they ... they ... I'm
sorry, Mac. I'm so sorry. She starts to cry.

It's okay, Sly. I could give a fuck about the money or the
rock. That shit doesn't matter. What matters is you. You're
hurt. I think we should take you to the hospital.

No! No hospital! Fuck that!

This is the first time any of us have ever heard Sly Girl raise her voice.

Okay, okay. Just relax. Mac looks over at me, eyebrows up, turns back to Sly. Is anything broken? Can you walk?

I don't know.

Do you want to try?

No. I want to die.

Mac sighs and daubs at the blood around Sly's nose.

Owww!

Sorry.

We're gonna kill those motherfuckers, Kayos says, pacing the room, her eyes hard and bright. Tell us what they looked like.

Sly starts to cry again, and I go kneel on the floor beside her head, look into her good eye. Sly, honey. Did they rape you?

She nods and hides her face in the couch, sobs racking her body.

We all look at each other. I see a tear slide down Kayos's face. Her fists are balled up and she seems to be vibrating.

Jesus, Mac says.

Cocksuckers! We'll chop their dicks off! Kayos kicks and slashes the air.

Maybe we should go to that walk-in clinic, Z mumbles.

I think we should definitely take her to the hospital. She needs to get tested, says Mac. She'll get the morning-after pill, probably some stitches, a cast, and whatever else—

I'm not going to the fuckin hospital so you can all just fuck off! Sly Girl screams between sobs.

Okay. Okay. Just relax. We're going to get you through this. Promise. I give her a tiny smile, then go to the kitchen and mix two parts vinegar with one part water in a plastic pop bottle. I don't know if it will do anything, but I figure it's better than nothing. I go back to the living room. Help me get her into the shower.

KAYOS

It's totally fucked up what happened to Sly Girl. I swear to God, I'm gonna kill the two fucks who did this to her.

Mercy and Mac put her in the shower. Then Mac gave me fifty bucks and sent me down to the 24-hour pharmacy to get her the morning-after pill.

Can I drive?

Do you have your licence?

I got my N.

Alright, go. Take Z with you.

The pharmacy is just around the corner. I eye up all the Oxycontin bottles behind the counter, and think about how much we could make selling those little gems on the street. I imagine I'm Matt Dillon's girlfriend in *Drugstore Cowboy*, and we just sweep the entire shelf into a pillowcase and take off. Then I remember why I'm there. I'm afraid I might be pregnant and need to get the morning-after pill. The white-haired pharmacist asks me to sign a form, and then he hands over the Plan B. I pay the cashier at the front. It's too easy. Jesus Christ, I wish I'd thought of this. Then I wouldn't have my stepdad's kid. But I was too young to know what to do then. I was barely thirteen.

Z buys a first-aid kit, some Polysporin, and acetaminophen with codeine. We zip back to the pad, and they've got Sly all tucked into bed. Mac and Mercy stand in the corner of the room. They stop talking when we come in. I sit on Sly's bed and pop the little pink pill out of the blister pack and tell her everything's gonna be okay. Watch her swallow it with water.

Her face is all puffed up like a koala bear, purply black bruises spreading around her eyes.

Z opens up the first-aid kit. What first?

Sly Girl struggles to pull up her shirt and removes a bloody washcloth, revealing a two-inch gash beneath her right breast.

I look away, feel the bile rise up the back of my throat. Swallow.

Yikes. Alright, let's clean that up and get some gauze on it, okay? Z says.

Uh-huh.

Z pours some clear liquid into the wound.

Sly Girl sucks her teeth.

We all suck our teeth.

Breathe, Z says.

It hurts to breathe.

Try humming.

What?

Humming. You know. Like a song.

What should I hum?

How bout, "You Are My Sunshine"? I say, and start humming it.

Z hums it too, then Mercy, then Mac. Finally, Sly Girl does too. We are all humming while Z tapes layers and layers of white absorbent bandages over Sly's wound until we can't see the dark blood oozing through anymore. Then she gets out a Q-tip and applies some Polysporin to the cuts on Sly Girl's face. Her hands are quick and careful. She's like pro-medic, yo. It's impressive. For real.

Here, take two of these and call me in the morning, Z says with a half-smile. She shakes two pills out of the bottle.

Wait. Mac grabs the bottle out of her hand. She can't have these.

Why not?

There's codeine in them.

Yeah, I know. That's why I got them.

Just give her another shot of whiskey.

Yeah, sure, she can wash the pills down with it.

Z, can I talk to you outside?

They go out of the room.

I look over at Mercy. Uh-oh, trouble in paradise.

Sly Girl half-laughs, and then moans.

Shh, just try to lay still, Mercy says. She goes to the window, raises the blind, and peeks out. Sly Girl moans again, coughs. Poor thing. She looks hella rough. We probably should have taken her to the hospital. For real. Obviously she needs something stronger than regular acetaminophen. I don't know what Mac's problem is. She can be a real bitch sometimes.

Can I talk to you alone for a minute? I took Z's wrist and pulled her outside Sly Girl's bedroom.

What the fuck, babe? It's just acetaminophen.

It's acetaminophen with codeine, Z.

So what?

So, Sly Girl is a heroin addict.

Is or was?

Same thing.

Z rolled her eyes at me, but she didn't know. She didn't know a goddamn thing about it. So? What? You think codeine is gonna make her relapse or some shit?

I nodded.

Oh, come on! You're not serious.

I've seen it happen before. When I was around eleven or twelve, my mom went straight. She was doing real good, clean for two, maybe three months, then she twisted her ankle, just stepped on it the wrong way, wearing her ridiculous platform shoes, and the doctor gave her T3s for the pain. That did it. Put the taste for opiates right back into her. Next morning, she was hobbling down Hastings, looking for a fix. But who would believe that? Who would even care?

We heard Sly Girl groan from inside the room.

I'm giving them to her. She was fucking *stabbed*, Mac. The girl's in pain. Her nose is broken, obviously. Maybe a rib. Who knows what else? I can't stand by and do nothing when I could be helping her. She twisted the knob and slipped through the door.

I stayed in the hallway for a second, listening to her gentle voice telling Sly she was gonna feel better real soon. I sighed and went into my room, closed the door. I clenched and unclenched my fists as I stared into the mirror. One thing was for certain, we were gonna find the guys who did this to her and we were going to make them sorry they'd ever been born.

My stomach growled, and I thought of my abandoned spaghetti. None of us had eaten. I ordered three large pizzas and waited by the door, chain-smoking.

MERCY

The four of us sat in the front room eating pizza and drinking Lucky Lager.

So ... ? Kayos said around a mouthful of Hawaiian.

So? Mac said.

What are we gonna do?

What do you mean?

Well, we're gonna fuck these motherfuckers up, right?

Mac laughed quietly and looked down at her plate. Yeah.

Well, alright! Let's make a plan then, yo.

Kayos was just like she'd been in elementary school, always looking to kick the shit out of somebody. I guess people don't really change.

That night we decided to let Sly Girl rest until she was ready to come out hunting with us. Later, we would find and abduct her attackers and make them get down on their knees and beg her for forgiveness. We would give them some kind of souvenir to remember us by. Maybe knife slashes across the cheeks. Maybe rip them a new asshole. Maybe both.

itz hard out here 4 a g. alwayz gotta B watchin yr bak. watchin yr friendz bak. watchin out 4 copz. watchin out 4 ppl wanna rob U, play U, rape U, $lay U. evrybudee wanna get paid. get laid. get made. evrybudee wanna be on top. cru$h U just 2 get dere. ju$t another day in da hood.

SLY GIRL

Layin in the filth of that alley, seein my own blood pool around my head, I thought I was dead, I really did. And if I wasn't already, I wanted to be. I couldn't move, couldn't speak. Felt like my insides had been rammed up into my throat. Everythin throbbing, aching, bleeding. I listened for their voices, but alls I could hear was static, like a TV channel that don't work. I just closed my eyes and hoped it would be over sooner than later. But it never was. It never, never was. I guess I blacked out for a while, I don't know for how long. When I opened my eyes again, there was a huge rat in my face, snifflin around my ear. Oh, man, it took everythin I had to roll over and away from it. The pain of a hundred knives shot through my body when I did. I wondered if I'd been stabbed. I couldn't breathe properly. I wished some junkie would come by and give me a pity shot. But no one came. I reached into my pocket and texted Mac. Then passed out again.

When I came to again, I was on the couch at home, wrapped in blankets, and my girls were gathered round me, their faces all twisted with worry. I hated what had happened, but I loved that they were there. They wanted to take me to the hospital, but I said no way. Hospital's where you go to die. Everyone from the rez who ever went to the hospital never came back. All of them died in there. Not even all old people either—lots of young people too. My cousin Mel died in hospital, my Auntie Linda, lots of people. Not me, though. Cuz I ain't goin. The girls wouldn't understand that, so I didn't bother explainin.

Plus it was hard to talk, like I was so outta breath, it felt like I'd just run across the city and back. Then I pictured myself in that weird German movie. I've got awesome bright red hair and I'm runnin away forever. The girls brung me some water so's I can talk better, and I said what they done to me. It wasn't the first time, but it was the worst. I felt all broken inside. Felt like shards of glass were all stuck up in me down there. Everythin hurt. Even my hair hurt. I wondered how much more of this life I could take, and I wished I could tie off right there on the couch, jam a needle in my arm and float away.

Mac and Mercy helped me get into the shower, and at first the water hurt. Felt like wasps stingin me all over. I felt dizzy and sick as I watched my blood swirl down the drain. My wrist felt like it had been smashed by a hammer, and I had a flash memory of one of them standin on it while the other one ... I threw up then and it went down the drain with everythin else.

Mercy helped me get out of the shower and wrapped a blue towel around me. You'll be alright in a little while, Sly Girl. You're a tough cookie.

Yeaah.

You tired?

Yeaah.

Let's get you into bed.

Okay.

Mercy helped me put on my pyjamas and get into bed like I was a little kid.

Mac came in and asked me how I was doin.

Been better, I said.

Yeah, I guess so. I'm so sorry this happened to you, Sly Girl. I feel awful.

It wasn't your fault, I whispered.

She shrugged. Maybe.

What's important now is that you rest and get well, Mercy said. But you might have a concussion so we're going to need to wake you up every couple of hours.

What?

Just to make sure, you know ...

What?

To make sure you don't fall into a coma.

Really?!

Don't worry. Just relax. We're going to look after you. She looked at Mac, and Mac nodded.

I closed my eyes and stared at the red blobs on the inside of my eyelids.

Sly?

Mmhmm?

Got you a magic pill. It was Kayos, holdin a pink pill and a glass of water out to me.

Pain killer?

Baby stopper.

KAYOS

After school on Monday, I went to Sport Chek and bought two steel bats. Then I took the bus down to the house on Cordova. Sly Girl was propped up on the couch watching *Scarface*. I asked her if she needed anything.

Yeaah.

What?

A new set of lungs.

I'll see what I can do. But no promises.

She laughed. Her breathing was raspy and stuttery. She had been stabbed that night in Crack Alley, and our best guess was that they'd punctured her lung. She still refused to go to the hospital, though, so we just hoped to hell it didn't get infected and did what we could to keep her comfortable.

Got a smoke?

Not for you.

Come on! she whined.

Seriously?

How bout a joint?

No fucking way are you smoking any-fucking-thing, Sly Girl! You want your fucking lungs to collapse? Fuck! Did your brain get damaged when you fell?

She turned away from me and stared at the TV screen.

Sorry.

She shrugged.

Are you in pain?

She nodded. We watched as Al Pacino smoked a cigar in a huge bubble bath.

I wouldn't mind seeing what's underneath those bubbles.

Sly giggled.

How bout I make you some weed tea?

She shrugged again, and I went into the kitchen to look for some cream.

Mac and Z were cleaning each other's tonsils in front of the fridge. I coughed loudly and they slowly drifted apart.

What's up, Kayos? Z said.

Yo.

Mac's face flushed pink, and she wouldn't meet my eyes. She took Z by the hand and they went into their room.

I wished I had someone to make out with. Not one of the girls, obviously, but someone ... hot. Someone my own age. I ground up a gram of weed and boiled the water. A vision of Roger getting out of the shower flooded my head. I don't know why. I didn't ever want to think of him like that. Ever. I squeezed my eyes shut to get him outta there. I thought of this guy from my high school, Ben McInnis. He was popular, a jock. Six foot two inches, crewcut, rugby shirts, dimples. He was not my type at *all*. He didn't know I existed, and even if he did, he would never, never kiss me. I left the tea to steep, went into the bathroom, and locked the door.

MERCY

It could have happened to any of us, that's what scared me. There was nothing we could have done. We told her not to go down there alone, and she did. But it wasn't anyone's fault. Everyone thinks that they can do it alone. Until something like this happens.

A couple days after it happened I went to an ATM in Gastown and relieved a fat suit of $300 he would've wasted on bad cologne and titty magazines. Then I went to Mountain Equipment Co-op. I bought five cans of bear spray. I didn't steal it because the metal detector would have gone off and they had a handful of secret shoppers in there anyway. No point ruining my clean record now. The cashier gave me a look like, what's up with you, bear-trainer chick? But I kept my face blank and didn't say a word. Sure, we all had guns, but you can't just go around shooting people every week. Sooner or later, someone's going to start to notice. I still couldn't believe that Kayos had gotten away with murder, and I knew that eventually, it would come back to haunt us. That's the way this game works. No one ever really gets away with shit like that. Maybe for a while, but not forever.

The mace came to $112. I got a falafel for lunch and brought the rest of the cash home to Mac for our condo fund. Someday soon, we'd be set up sweet in West Van, sipping lattes on our balcony, overlooking Burrard Inlet, the Lions Gate Bridge.

I gave every girl a can and showed them all how to spray it. And don't use it if the wind's blowing toward you!

No shit, Sherlock, Mac said.

I stuck out my tongue at her and she made a pig face.

A timer went off in the kitchen, and we both reached for our guns.

Z stood up. Who wants pie?

I do! Kayos jumped up and ran into the kitchen. The timer quit beeping. Mac and I looked at each other.

Never heard the timer go off before.

Something about it made me think of a bomb.

Me too.

Sly Girl giggled at us from the couch. You guys are paranoid.

Z and Kayos brought out apple pie and plates. They took a piece to Sly Girl, and the rest of us sat around the table and ate it all up.

This is delicious, babe! Mac said.

Yeah, it's hella good, Z.

It was really easy to make.

You know what? Sly Girl said. I think I'm ready to go looking for them guys tonight.

Yes! Kayos yelled, her knees bouncing up and down.

Are you sure? I asked her. We don't have to. It can wait until you're feeling better.

Totally, said Mac. There's no rush.

Nah. We should go now. Tonight. Before I forget what they look like.

Alright. If you're sure.

We are gonna fuck up their shit, Sly. No doubt.

Yeaah.

Hells, yeah.

We all punched knuckles. I wondered if the others had the same heavy feeling in their guts as I did.

SLY GIRL

It happened five days ago. My breathin was gettin better and the swellin in my face had gone down, but I still felt like someone had taken a blowtorch to my bones. Z made me a wrist splint, and I knew I wasn't gonna have a baby, so that was the biggest thing out of the way. A part of me was still afraid though. I locked myself in the bathroom and looked in the mirror for a long time. My face was fucked. Broken nose, two black eyes turning blue-green, split lip, cut on my cheek, cuts on my forehead, plus my eye that was already a write-off. My face couldn't possibly get any more fucked up. I felt real sad for a minute, and thought I might cry, but there was just nothin there no more to cry about. It was a different feeling inside now, like dry and sharp, angry. Okay, Sly Girl, I said to myself. This is it. If you ain't ready now, you ain't never gonna be ready. I went back out to the kitchen where the girls sat at the table eating pie. Let's go get those fuckin assholes.

Tonight?

Yeaah.

Yeeeeooow! No one fucks with a Black Rose!

You fuck with the Black Roses, the Black Roses are gonna fuck with you!

We gonna whup some ass to-night, bitches! For real!

Mercy, Mac said. We're gonna need an SUV for this.

I'm on it.

A few hours later, we all piled into a black Explorer. I got to sit shotgun. They wrapped me in blankets and told me not to get out of the car no matter what. Mac and Kayos each held a bat across their laps. Z had a roll of duct tape. We all had our guns. And the bear spray.

My heart beat faster as we got closer to Crack Alley. The streets were shiny with rain. Mercy slowed down as we passed Pigeon Park. Two guys huddled on a bench, tryin to light a pipe.

Is that them?

I squinted through the darkness. I don't know. I can't tell. It's too dark.

Kayos sighed. Tell us what they look like.

Well, they were both skinny. You know, cracked-out like.

Yeah, and?

They were both wearing black.

Uh-huh.

One of them had a toque on. A black toque.

Come on, Sly! You just described ninety-nine percent of the guys down here! How the fuck are we supposed to find them off that!

Take it easy, Kayos. I'm sure she'll recognize them when she sees them, Mercy said.

The other guy had a Canucks hat on. It was blue.

Alright. Well, at least that's something. What kind of hair did they have?

I dunno.

Yo, try to *remember!*

I squeezed my eyes shut. Why was she being so mean to me? It should've been *her* out there slingin that night. And me all cozy up in the restaurant. I felt bad for thinkin that, but it just wasn't fair, you know?

Let's cruise past Oppenheimer, Mac said.

Everyone on the street looked mean that night. The rain began to fall in thick sheets of grey, and I couldn't see shit.

Is that them? Z pointed to two guys standing around a grocery cart with a bunch of other skids. One wore a black toque, the other a Canucks cap.

I rolled down the window to get a better look.

Well?

Yeaah, that's them. I felt my throat closing up. Suddenly, I couldn't breathe.

Mercy reached for my hand. It's going to be okay, Sly. We're not going to let them hurt you again, okay? You stay in the car. Don't move, alright?

I nodded.

She turned around to the back seat. Ready?

Born ready.

Let's do this.

I watched through the windshield as the four of them approached the guys, actin all friendly. The guys were smilin and laughin and snakin their arms around Mercy and Mac. I swallowed some puke that came up my throat. The girls led them away from the group of people they were with and toward the SUV. I saw how Mercy and Mac patted the guys down, but made it look like they were just casually touching them. It was like they were pros at this. They led them around to the other side of the vehicle, I guess so their friends couldn't see, then Mac, Mercy, and Kayos pulled their guns. Z stuck duct tape over the guys' mouths, and wrapped up their wrists behind their backs. Then Kayos took out her bear spray and sprayed it right at their faces. The guys jerked around, trying to wipe their eyes on their shoulders, each other's backs.

Mercy opened the back door.

Get in the fucking truck, Kayos said.

They got in.

Don't move, you fucking maggot. Kayos levelled her gun at Canucks guy's forehead, while Z wrapped his ankles together with duct tape, then did the other guy.

They were whimpering and moaning as I stared at them in the rear-view mirror. Part of me wanted them dead, and part of me didn't want to be doin this at all. My heart was explodin in my chest. I held my head in my hands and tried to make my breathing normal.

MERCY

I backed into our driveway and let the girls drag Sly's attackers out of the SUV. They used the sheet method, like Mac and I had with old Blue Eyes. Then I parked a few blocks away and ran back to our house.

When I got back, they had carried the guys down to the basement, and Kayos and Mac were wailing on them with their new bats. Sly Girl sat huddled in a corner, trembling. The single bare light bulb that hung from the ceiling gave all of us long, weird shadows, and darkened the circles beneath our eyes. I stepped in and gave both guys some good hard kicks to the stomach and ribs. They cowered on the cold cement and tried to shield their heads with their arms.

Get in here, Sly Girl! Kayos yelled.

Sly shook her head.

Come on, it feels good! She bashed the toque dude in the face, and his eyes went crossed. She laughed and ground the bat into his belly, hard. What do you want us to do to them, Sly?

Sly shook her head, shrugged. I dunno.

Yo, come on! This is for you! This is your chance for revenge! She turned back to the dudes. You wanna fuck with the Black Roses? Hey? You filthy pieces of shit. You're gonna get fucked. Here, hold this. She handed me the bat and raced upstairs.

I took a few cracks at their taped-up hands, because I knew that would hurt.

Z kicked them both in the junk, and they screamed like drowning puppies. They were both crying and pleading through their duct tape. The skin around their eyes was red and puffy from the mace.

Shut up! Mac yelled. You think it's okay to attack someone? Leave her for dead in an alley? Thought you were gonna get away with that? You fuckin idiots. You're worthless bags of skin and don't deserve to live. She whacked each of them across the face with the bat.

Kayos ran back down the stairs holding my curling iron like a sword. Her eyes were wild, and she was grinning like a mental case. She plugged the curling iron in, took the bat back from me, and started smashing their kneecaps to smithereens.

I watched as the curling iron began to glow red hot.

Pull down their pants, Kayos said to me and Z.

We looked at each other.

Do it!

Kayos … what are you—

An eye for an eye, bitches.

I looked at Mac standing in the shadows.

Yo! What are you waiting for? Kayos yelled. Pull their fucking pants down right fucking now!

I pulled down toque dude's jeans and boxers while Z did the same to Canucks guy. I stood back and stared with disgust at their pimpled hairy asses. I felt like gagging, but I swallowed it back. Sly Girl was rocking herself back and forth in the corner and staring at the wall. Her eyes looked like they had a layer of waxed paper over them.

You messed with the wrong girl, Kayos said. And then, she did it.

Toque guy screamed and flailed around on the ground. He bashed his head against the concrete floor.

Oh my God, Z said.

Kayos, Mac said.

When she slid the curling iron out, smoke was coming out his asshole. He lay motionless on the floor, his eyes closed. You could smell the burning flesh, and then I did gag.

Kay—

She rammed the curling iron up the other guy, and he let out a high-pitched, inhuman noise. He bucked and humped against the ground, but that probably only made it worse. I covered my ears and looked around the room. It seemed like everything was happening in slow motion. Sly Girl rocked, covering her eyes with her hands. Mac and Z stared, their faces pale as concrete. Kayos removed the curling iron and plunged it into him again and again. You fucker! You fucker! You fuck!

I went over to her. Tears were streaming down her face. I touched her shoulder, and her arm went limp. She turned away and sat down on the floor with a thud. She put her head in her hands and sobbed. The curling iron was still sticking out of the guy's ass. It made a sizzly sucking sound as I pulled it out. I set it down on the floor. Neither of the guys were moving.

Jesus Christ. Let's get them outta here, Mac said, nodding to me.

I made my way back to the Explorer like I was walking through Jell-O. Z, Mac, and Kayos loaded the guys back into the SUV and I drove around for a few minutes till we spotted an open dumpster with no one around. I backed up to it, and the five of us heaved their bodies into the dumpster, let the lid fall closed with a bang.

No one said a word on the way home.

We all flopped on the couches when we got back to the house. Kayos started rolling a joint. That was awesome, she laughed.

That was way too fucked up, I said.

Yo, we're a gang, right? We gotta represent. We gotta pull a little hardcore shit out every now and then. It's the only way we're gonna survive out here. For real. Right, Mac?

Mac pressed her lips together and nodded slowly.

Anyway, we didn't give them anything they didn't deserve. Feel better, Sly?

Sly shrugged. I dunno.

I smoked two joints with them, then went into the bathroom to shower and gargle with Scope. The smell of charred flesh had lodged itself in the back of my throat, and as much as I tried, I couldn't get rid of it.

MAC

I didn't know whether to be proud or ashamed of my girls that night. Yeah, they'd shown they were hard—without a doubt—but now, we were just as evil as the crack fiends we'd blackened.

But like my Uncle Hank always says, what goes around comes around.

It had been confirmed, we weren't playing no kids' game. The Black Roses were the real McCoy, bad-ass gangster motherfuckers.

The crack fiends were still alive when we dumped them. I know because I checked for a pulse in both their ropy necks. That meant that if they didn't die in the dumpster that night, they could come after us. We'd blinded them with the pepper spray so they wouldn't have been able to see where we were going and wouldn't know where the house was. Unless they had excellent mental maps, and, let's face it, crackheads aren't really known for their spatial memory. But they'd seen all of our faces, which meant none of us was safe.

It was time to beef up security at our little house on Cordova. The cost of cheap gats had tripled recently because of a Mexican gun-run that had gone sideways. I was thinking more along the lines of recruiting a new member, a canine G.

VANCOUVER

They are slippery shadows in the night. They are beasts in bandanas. They are ruthless. They are cunning. They are brutally violent. They are born ready. They are armed. They are taught to kill or be killed. They are wanted. They are marked. They are hunted like dogs. They are respected and feared. They are angry. They are hungry. They are not taking no for an answer. They are trained professionals. They are numb to suffering. They are harder than the hardest. They are self-reliant, self-sufficient, and self-serving. They are entitled to everything. They are afraid of nothing. They are heavily armed and extremely dangerous. They are seeking revenge on the world. They are here to search and destroy. They are not sorry. They are the future. They are children, lost to my city, doing what is necessary to survive.

SLY GIRL

I think it's gonna rain forever.

when Mac came hOme w/ a dawg i nearlee choked on my apple!!! i nevr wuda thought $he wuz a dawg per$un. den dere wuz di$ lil thing $kittering all ovr da hou$e. but he wuz $o cute & $o pre$hu$ & ju$t wanted 2 love u$ all up. da look on $ly Girl'$ face, man, U $huda $een it. it wa$ lyke $umthing in$yde her ju$t crAKed open & $he $myled w/ her whole bodee. he ran in circlez cheking all of u$ out, $niffing our a$$e$. he ran around evry room, den came bak & peed in da middle of da kitchen.

Oh Jesus, Mac $ed, handz on her hipz.

Don't worry. I'll get it, $ly Girl $ed, grabbing a wad of paper towelz. It's alright. It's alright, she laffed. It's just pee.

da dawg wuz a tan pit bull puppee & da mo$t adorable thing i have evr laid eyez on. i wi$hed he wuz all myne, but i knew dat Mac had gotten him 4 $ly Girl. & aftr wat $he'd been thru, $he de$erved it.

after $he cleened up hiz pee, $ly $cooped him up into her armz & nuzzled into hiz face. It's okay. Don't worry, little doggie. I'm not mad at you. $he lookd @ Mac. Do we get to keep him?

we all looked @ Mac.

What do you think?

Yeah! we all $ed & gathrd around $ly Girl 2 pet da lil $tinker. i watched Kayo$ out da cornr of my eye az $he cooed & babee-talked to da dawg. her face $oftened & it wuz lyke all her rage ju$t melted away. @ dat moment, i could imagine her az a lil kid, wearing a pink frillee dre$$, $kipping rope, a long wayz away from da hardcore G $he wuz 2day.

where'd U get him? i a$ked Mac.

A breeder my uncle knows on the island.

Wow, he's a purebred? Kayo$ $ed.

Of course. A hundred percent American Pit Bull Terrier. Got his papers in the car. His Mom was a champion fighter.

Sick, yo.

How much did he cost? Mercy a$ked.

Enough so that we have to take really good care of him, and not let anything happen to him. Ever. Agreed?

How much? Mercy $ed.

Three.

Hundred?

Grand.

Mercy whi$tled thru her teeth. Shit, Mac, don't you think this is something we should've discussed as a gang before you went out and spent all that money?

Mac blinked az if $he'd been $lapped in da face. I wanted to surprise you guys, I...I mean, we need this dog for other reasons, Mercy.

What reasons?

Security, for one.

Oh yeah? What's it going to do? Lick intruders to death?

we all looked @ da dawg being cradled lyke a lil babee, licking $ly's fingr lyke it wuz a auage. Mercy wuz ryte. it wa$n't eXactly da mo$t viciou$ thing on 4 legz.

Well, that's why I got a puppy, so we could train it to be

friendly with us and mean with everyone else.

Mercy sighed & looked on az me, Kayos & $ly $mothrd da pup w/ luv & ki$$e$.

Alright, you're right. I'm sorry, Mac $ed. We should've talked about it. Made the decision together. But if you really don't want him, I'm sure the breeder will take him back.

$ly Girl looked up from da dawg, her face set 2 panik mode.

Let's have a vote, Mac $ed.

Mercy rolled her eyez.

All in favour of keeping the dog, raise your hand.

all handz $hot up, Xcept Mercyz.

All opposed?

I just think we should have talked about it first, that's all.

But you're okay with keeping him? Right? $ly Girl a$ked. Right, Mercy?

Mercy gazed @ da dawg.

Right?

As long as it doesn't piss in my room or bite me.

He won't! $ly Girl $ed. I promise.

And it can't chew up our shoes either. There's easily ten grand worth of shoes and boots in this house.

He won't wreck our shoes. I'll make sure. I'll put them all in the closet and keep the door closed.

Alright, Mercy $hrugged. Whatever.

Oh thank you, thank you! Thank you! $ly Girl held da dawg up 2 Mercyz face. I ruv roo Mercy.

Mercy rolled her eyez, $hook her hed, & walked outta da room.

wat R we gonna name him? i a$ked. all of u$ $tared @ da dawg. his front left paw wuz wyte & so wuz hiz che$t. hiz hed lolled bak & he wuz grinning thru hiz black lipz.

How about Scooby? Mac $ed.

Nah. That's not a good name for a G-Dog. Too cutesy, $ed Kayo$.

how bout Thug? i $ed.

Thug. Come here, Thug. Thuggy Thuggy Thug Thug. Yeah, I like it, Kayo$ $ed. What do you think, Sly?

Thug. Yeah, it's a good name. $he laffed az da dawg licked her hand.

Mac?

Seems appropriate, $he $myled.

Thug it is. Kayo$ $cratched behind hiz earz.

& $o, the Black Ro$e$ got itz 6th membr.

SLY GIRL

There were tons of dogs on the rez, but they didn't belong to no one. Not really. Some people would say, Oh that's my dog. He's mine, leave him be. But those dogs didn't belong to nobody, and every other year the SPCA would come round and shoot almost all of them. I wished that one of them could be mine. I wished I could save just one. There was this little golden dog that liked to be petted when she was just a pup. I used to brush out her fur with my cousin's hairbrush. Ha ha. Named her Goldilocks, my cousin and me. But when she got a bit older, she didn't come round no more. Just stayed with the pack, wrestlin, carryin bloody squirrels around in her mouth, causin a ruckus at night with the others. One day, the SPCA came and loaded her and some other dogs into the back of a big white van, and I never seen her again.

But now, finally, *finally*, I have a dog. Well, he isn't just mine, he's all of ours, but I like to think of him as mine. Thug's a pure-bred American Pit Bull Terrier, the colour of sand, and he's probably the cutest, smartest, lovingest dog in the wide world. Mac brought home a bunch of books for me from the library about how to train dogs and care for pit bulls. I flipped through a couple of them, but I don't really like to read much, so I just looked at the pictures. Mercy got Thug a black leather collar studded with spikes and a thick black leather leash. Real bad-ass, eh, ha ha. Perfect. She asked me how his trainin was comin along as she buckled his new collar.

Um, not bad. I think he's gettin good at only goin to the bathroom outside.

Uh-huh...

And, he comes when you call him.

Yeah, usually.

Am I...am I sposed to teach him to attack?

I guess that's the idea, eventually. But you can start with just simple stuff like heel, sit, stay, roll over, that kind of thing. Hey, have you thought of taking him to a class?

What do you mean?

Like a doggie training class, where you go once or twice a week and there's an instructor and other dogs come and—

I didn't really know things like that existed.

Oh yeah, sure. I always overhear the doggie-purse chicks in the mall talking about their obedience classes, she laughed. I'll talk to Mac about getting you signed up for one. What do you think?

Uh, sure, I guess. If you think it would help.

I'm sure it will. She reached down and petted Thug's head, and he licked her jeans and nuzzled into her leg.

I couldn't imagine him ever attackin anybody or even being fierce. But I guess that's why Mac got him, to protect us.

PART 3
DOWN FOR LIFE

KAYOS

I've wanted a dog my whole entire life, but we could never get one because jerk-ass Roger is allergic. Well, I'm allergic to *him*. We should get rid of him and let a dog move in. Seriously. Anyway, Thug is totally awesome, even though his head is huge and he bumps into everything and knocks over whatever's in his path, and when he wags his tail and it hits your leg it's like you're getting whipped with a stick. But he can't help it.

Sly Girl was supposed to train him up, right, so she'd have something to focus on and hopefully get out of her depression or whatevs. But I think he listens to me more. I like taking him for walks around the hood because instead of giving me their usual sneer or *Heyyy girl*, people actually give me respect. For real. They take one look at Thug and keep walking straight ahead, maybe give me a little nod. Like nobody's gonna mess, you know? It's nice. Really nice. He's getting hella big really fast and kinda just pulls us along instead of heeling like he's supposed to.

Sly Girl is maybe gonna take him to doggie training classes to get him whipped into shape. Because it's hard work training a dog, you know? It's not like a little kid where you can just make them do whatever you say. A dog is different. Especially if they're big, like Thug is. As lame as it sounds, I sorta wanted to go to doggie training class too, but it was on Tuesdays, and I have my mixed martial arts class that night, and I can't give that up because I'd probably go nuts without it.

I've been spending a lot of time at the Cordova house,

though, just to be around Thug and my girls and all the action downtown. A part of me knows I should be at home with Laura, getting her dressed, giving her baths, feeding her, playing with her. But, I mean, I'm fifteen years old. There's gonna be time for all that junk later. Right now, I just want to party.

I never really thought I'd be in a gang. I mean, I thought all those colours and rags and shit were pretty dumb, kid's stuff, you know? But the Black Roses aren't like that. I mean, we're in this to win it. We're not just screwing around like so many wannabes out there. We're too legit to quit! For real. And now that I'm with them, it's like I was always meant to be part of it, this thing of ours. They're like my family now, yo. Seriously. Down for life, baby. Down for life.

SLY GIRL

I took Thug to dog trainin over in Yaletown. Man, it's just a few blocks away, but it's like a whole different universe over there. All these blonde sparkly chicks with their Chihuahuas, the slick-haired yuppies with their Labs and Whippets, and the wannabe bad guys with their Boxers and Rotties, blue-haired oldies with their Bichons, Cockapoos, mini-whatevers. I'm the only one with a pit bull, and everyone kinda shies away from me and Thug, eh, like we're gonna bite their heads off or somethin. Thug isn't the worst dog in class, but he ain't the best either. He gets real excited about everythin and likes to sniff everybody's butt, dogs and people. It's hard for me to keep hold of him when he gets it in his head that he's goin somewheres and he'll just drag me along behind him. I don't really even stand much of a chance, eh.

Our teacher is Brady. Brady says I need to block Thug with my body and make him know it's not okay to go anywheres when I don't want him to. Brady says pit bulls are super intelligent, but they need a lot of work and training to get them to behave how you want them to. When me and Thug walk around the room, the ladies scoop up their little puffball dogs and hold them in their laps so Thug won't step on their heads. He doesn't mean to step on their heads, but he's just so big and excited that he does sometimes anyways. We've got a ways to go, but this week he did sit-stay and didn't move for a full ten seconds, even though there was a dog treat two feet away. Ten seconds is a long time for a dog, eh, but Thug didn't get up until I told him to. I was so proud.

MERCY

When I got home tonight, the worst thing that could have happened had. Our stuff was all over the house. The coke was gone. The crack was gone. The scale was gone. The safe was gone.

I felt sick inside. Our entire life savings. Everything we'd worked so hard for. Gone. The Vipers sign was spray-painted in red on the wall by the door. Those fuckers. We didn't owe them shit. And they took from us everything they could carry.

I sat down on my bed and called Mac. Where the fuck was everybody? There was always someone home. Mac didn't answer. I swore and threw my phone across the room and squeezed my pillow. I felt like I couldn't breathe. My chest tightened and seized. Maybe I was having a heart attack. I lay down on my bed because I remembered hearing once that if you were having a heart attack you should lay down. I stared up at the ceiling. It looked wavy through my tears. Now what were we supposed to do? We had practically every dollar we owned in there. For our condo. Our dream home. Now we had nothing.

What was the point of having five members and a purebred pit-fucking-bull if we couldn't even guard our assets? Useless. Totally useless. It was all gone. We might as well not have done any of it. And what could I do about it? Call the cops?

Oh, hello, excuse me officer, but my kilo of coke and all the money I've saved from selling it, stealing cars, and pulling bank frauds has gone missing. Do you think you could help me get it back?

Fucking hopeless.

I went to the toilet and dry heaved for a while but nothing came up. I couldn't remember the last time I'd felt this awful. Just when I thought we finally had a handle on things, just when I thought we were finally going to get out of this rat hole, it all went down the shitter. Typical.

I called Mac again. She answered, breathless and laughing. I could hear Z in the background saying something about candyfloss.

Where are you?

Just hanging out with Z. We're on the steps of the art gallery.

Come home right now.

Why? What's up?

We've been robbed.

Oh no.

Oh yes.

How bad?

Everything.

Fuuuck. I could hear the catch in her throat. The shuffling of material as she stood up. We gotta go, she said to Z. Are you okay, Merce?

I don't know. This is bad.

Did you see anyone there?

It was the Vipers. They left their sign on the wall.

What? Fucking Cyco! Aarrgh!

I knew they wouldn't let us go so easily. But this is—

You're the only one home?

Yeah.

Okay, just sit tight. We're on our way.

I dropped my phone, put my head in my hands, and cried. For the first time in years, I cried.

What happened? What's wrong? Z scrambled to get her sketchbook into her bag and catch up with me.

The Vipers robbed us.

Aw, *shiiit*.

Come on. We gotta get home.

She grabbed my hand and hustled along beside me. We didn't often hold hands in public, but right then, it was good to have somebody to hold on to. My mind spun with a thousand thoughts. Everything. Gone. What should we do? What *could* we do? Should I call Hank? Where the fuck had everyone been? Why wasn't someone at home? What about the dog? Did they take the dog, too?

When I opened the door to our house and saw the coffee table flipped on its side, the empty space where the stereo had been, and all of our electronics, CDs, and DVDs gone, I felt a piercing pain in my heart. So, it was true.

I looked at Z. Her dark eyes glazed over, and she whistled through her teeth as she took in the trashed room. She gave me a hug, but there was nothing she could do to fix it.

Mercy?

I'm in here.

We went to her room. She sat on the bed and wiped at her eyes. Eyeliner was smeared like black ribbons across her temples. I went to her and held her.

It's all gone, she sobbed into my hair.

At least they left the TV, I said.

Yeah, because it's not worth anything, she said through her tears.

This is fucked up, Z said from the doorway, arms crossed over her chest.

Mercy's dresser drawers had been dumped out and her clothes were all over the room. They took all my jewellery, she sobbed. Those fucking bastards. This is all I have left!

She gestured to the gold hoop earrings and chain she wore.

Where was everyone? Why wasn't anyone home?

You and Z were out, Kayos is at school, Sly Girl's out slinging, and I was scouting cars.

Where's Thug?

She shrugged. I guess Sly Girl takes him with her.

Christ.

Z left the room. Mercy and I stared at each other, both expecting the other to say it was all a big joke. April Fool's! Ha ha! Gotcha! But neither of us was saying that. This was for real.

They unbolted the safe, Mercy said. Took the whole fuckin thing.

What? I jumped up to go check. There were four holes in the floor where the safe had been. Jesus, fuck! I wanted to punch something. Break something. Kill something. But more than that, I wanted our five-hundred K back. I could handle the jewellery, electronics, and the key of coke being gone, but not the cash. Not our entire life savings. Not that. Anything but that. I felt like I'd been punched in the stomach as I realized that it was all gone. The Vipers had fucked us over royally. Bye-bye condo. Bye-bye ever getting out from under the Downtown Eastside.

KAYOS

After math class, I checked my cell. There was a text from Mac: 911 meeting 2nite. Uh-oh. This couldn't be good. I couldn't sit through three more classes wondering what it was about. I left school and hopped on the next train down to Waterfront Station. The cherry blossoms were out, and they drifted around my head like pink confetti as I half-ran, half-walked toward the house. It was a beautiful spring day. What the hell could the problem be? I just hoped no one was hurt. That Sly hadn't relapsed and OD'd, that Z hadn't been busted again. I hoped Thug was okay. But whatever it was, we would deal with it. We were the Black Roses. Together, we could handle anything.

MERCY

Maybe I deserve all this. Maybe I deserve much, much worse.

Now, when I shut my eyes, all I can see are his ice-blue eyes. They are burned into my brain.

I could stand at the top of the Lookout Tower and yell *I'm sorry* at the top of my lungs a hundred billion times. I could lie down on the road at the exact spot I hit him and wait for my punishment. I could stow away in a shipping container and wake up in Japan or India or Australia and start a new life. But it wouldn't change what I did. Nothing can.

Well, that sucks, sweetie, but, you know, it's all part of the game. Hank covered the mouthpiece and asked someone if they had any more appointments today. Then he told them to go home. Sorry, what were you saying?

I just feel like such an idiot, you know? I mean, I thought we had it covered with a safe and a dog, but ... but that was fucking stupid. Why didn't I just open a bank account?

Well, you can't blame yourself, darlin. You just have to learn from it and move forward. You won't make the same mistake again. Sometimes you play the game, and sometimes the game plays you. That's just how it is.

We almost had enough for a condo. We were so close.

I felt a lump building in the back of my throat.

We lost *everything*, Hank. Everything. What the hell are we supposed to do now?

Well, I'll tell ya what you're not gonna do, you're not gonna mope around feeling sorry for yourself. You're gonna get right back on your feet and figure out a way to make it all back again. Look, I'll see to it that you get set up with your first couple orders, and you can start selling Tupperware again this weekend. Hank was always paranoid about drug-talk over the phone, for good reason, I guess. He had a lot to lose.

Thanks.

Hey, no sweat. Listen, you and your little book club can get creative now. There are ways to reel in big fish without spending years collecting sardines. Know what I mean?

I think so.

Good. Well, I'll talk to my friend tonight and get you sorted out.

Thanks a million, Hank.

Hang in there, kiddo. It'll turn out alright, you'll see. Gotta go, my next appointment's here. Whew, she's a fox. Bye.

Big fish. Get creative. Hank was right, we could pull one big con and make just as much money as we did spending hours and hours cooking, chopping, and slinging crack. But what could we do that was low-risk and high-reward?

I went for a walk to clear my head, get some fresh air. A wrecking ball was demolishing a building down the way. I stopped across the street and watched it come down, brick by brick, just falling in on itself. A crowd gathered on the sidewalk with me, and we all watched as this ugly little building was put out of its misery. I lit a smoke, and a junkie beside me asked me for one and I handed it to her, passed her my lighter.

It's kinda like watching a car accident, eh?

Yeah, it is, I said.

What's that about, anyways? she asked, scratching a sore on her face.

What's what about?

How come we're so drawn to car crashes and shit like this? She gestured to all the people who had stopped to watch the demolition.

I don't know. Curiosity, I guess.

It's more than that, though, she said, exhaling smoke from the corner of her mouth. It's like watching our own lives in slow motion.

VANCOUVER

I am constantly being destroyed. I am constantly being created. I am a vision of the past, present, and future. They say I am 125 years old, but I contain 8,000 years of human history.

I am a stinking, shining, gorgeous, awful manifestation of all the joys and fears, all the fantasies and illusions of every person who has ever stepped inside me. I am a concrete forest. I am a metallically realized dream. I am the City of Glass. The City of Tears. The Broken City. I am the Liveable City. World Class. I am Raincouver, Hongcouver, and No Fun City. I am Lotusland. Shangri-La. I am Hollywood North, the intersection of aspiration and desire. I am ground zero of hope. I am your last refuge and your final destination. I am the Terminal City, where everything that ends begins.

MERCY

I know we didn't owe them anything, and I can't believe they would fuck us over like that. But what does it really matter now? Our stuff is gone, and it's never coming back.

I went to the store to steal us some junk food because that usually helps me feel better when really shitty things happen. When I got home, Sly Girl, Mac, and Z were smoking a blunt and watching a movie on TV. At least we still had the TV.

You got some more weed? I asked, reaching for the joint.

Yeah, Hank's guy dropped by, Mac said.

That's good, I guess.

Yeah.

He fronted us?

Yeah.

How much?

Just an ounce. Don't worry. It'll move fast.

Cool. Want some ice cream? I held up the two tubs of Häagen-Dazs I'd managed to slip in my bag.

Fuckin rights. Mac leapt up and ran into the kitchen to grab spoons.

Z laughed and reached for the tub of Rocky Road.

I pushed Thug off the couch and settled in beside Sly Girl, careful not to bump her broken spots.

Here. Mac plunked down on the other side of me and handed me a spoon.

Thanks.

No, thank *you*.

Sly Girl giggled.

What are you guys watching?

Trapped.

What's going on?

Courtney Love and Kevin Bacon kidnapped this little girl for a million-dollar ransom, Mac said.

Huh.

Yeah. Mac met my eyes and hers flashed bright, and I knew we were thinking the exact same thing.

Not a bad idea, actually.

Too bad we don't know any rich people with little kids, Mac said.

Actually, we do.

KAYOS

I burst through the door expecting the worst. The girls were sitting around the living room, a nearly empty case of beer in the middle of the floor. Thug was curled up on the couch with his nose in Sly Girl's lap.

Yo, what's going on? What happened?

You're here! Mercy said.

Yeah, I left school. Now tell me what the hell's going on.

We were robbed, Mac said.

Oh shit! How bad?

They took everything.

Seriously?

Everyone nodded.

I sank onto the couch. The cash?

Yep.

The coke?

Everything.

Motherfuckers. Any idea who it was?

Mercy pointed to a red spray-painted mess on the wall. It was the Vipers symbol with a crown on top.

Mother*fuckers*.

Yep.

This is bad. This is really bad.

But it could be worse, Z said, cracking a beer. We've got each other. And we've got our health. She reached over and patted Thug's bum.

Somebody's been watching too much Oprah, Mercy said.

Z flicked a beer cap at her, stuck out her tongue.

So, what are we gonna do? How much did we have in the safe?

Almost five hundred, Mac said.

Okay, well, that's not so bad. Yo, we can make that back tonight, easy.

Thousand.

Oh.

Mac nodded, biting her lower lip.

Oh, *God*. It's gonna take another year to make all that back!

Maybe not, Mac said. We've been talking about some different strategies for our economic recovery.

The others laughed. I could tell they'd been boozing hard all afternoon. Nothing was funny about this situation. Everything we owned had just walked out the door. I wanted to cry.

Mac patted my shoulder. We've got—

No, no. Let me guess what you're gonna say. We cowboy up and get right back out there. It's all part of the game, right? I said.

Well, yeah, sort of. But we got a new plan to make our money back. Aside from the ATMs, cars, and dealing. Something big, a one-off. It's low-risk, high-reward.

Yeah? What is it?

Mac grabbed a beer, twisted off the cap, and handed it to me. Mercy's got an idea.

I took a swig and looked at Mercy, her bare feet up on the coffee table, fingers steepled over her belly, her shiny black hair loose, cascading over her shoulders. What is it? I asked.

A kidnapping, Mercy said.

Really?

Really.

You're not serious.

Serious as a fucking heart attack.

For real?

For ransom.

A kid?

Uh-huh. It'd be super easy.

But we'd need someone on the inside, Mac said. Everyone looked at me.

Whose kid? My skin felt hot and prickly. I didn't know where this was heading, but I was getting that heavy, squishy feeling in my guts.

Your sister, Mercy said.

Laura?

She nodded, her face smug.

Oh, guys, I don't know. That's ...

A brilliant, foolproof idea?

Um ...

Pure genius?

I don't know. I—

Okay, let me tell you something, Kayos. Mercy put her feet on the floor and leaned forward, hands on her thighs. This is our only shot at making that money back in one go. No one has to get hurt, alright? Hell, it's hardly even illegal since she's your sister and all; it'll be like we're babysitting her for the afternoon.

It's just that—

Kayos? Down for life, remember? She pulled back her shirt to show her black rose tattoo and the others did the same.

I sighed and took another gulp of beer. Alright, give me the deets. Yo, seriously, how in the hell do you think this is even gonna work?

MERCY

Yes, I'm a bad brown bitch, let it be known. No Mercy. It would be my biggest theft yet, a human being. The greatest part was, since we had Kayos on the inside, it was risk-free. Mac and I talked it out all afternoon from every angle and analyzed every little thing that could possibly go wrong. We drew up a schedule, a timeline, and a map of our locations. We had every detail laid out.

Is this crazy? I asked Mac.

Yep. But it's also kinda genius.

Is it going to work?

Without a doubt.

The hard part was convincing Kayos. The whole actual kidnapping thing would probably be a cakewalk compared to that.

Look, it's a simple plan, I told her. We'll do up the ransom note and be ready to come and get her as soon as your parents go out.

What about me?

You'll be there. In the house. Say you fell asleep watching TV or whatever.

They're not gonna fall for that.

Sure they will, why wouldn't they?

It just seems too convenient. They'll think—

Don't worry. They'll be so upset they won't put it together.

And you're not gonna hurt her, right? Nothing's gonna happen to her…

Come on, Kayos! What do you take us for? We may be

gangster-ass muthafuckas, but we're not child abusers.

Yo, you gotta promise me that nothing's gonna happen to her, Mercy. Otherwise I'm out. For real. I'm not—

I promise.

Swear on your life.

I swear on my father's grave. My mother's too.

And on your life.

I swear on my life.

All of you. Promise. Kayos looked around the room like a cornered cat.

Z held up two fingers. Scout's honour.

I'm not fucking around, Z! Kayos leapt off the couch. If anything, *anything* happens to her I'll—

Chill, Kay, said Mac. Just chill. We're not gonna let anything happen to her. If she's your sister, she's our sister too. Okay? We're family. We'll take good care of her, alright? Mac went to where Kayos stood in the centre of the room and put her hand under her chin, forcing Kayos to look up and meet her eyes. Alright?

Alright.

Besides, I asked her, won't it be nice to get a little coin out of that rich-ass douchebag stepfather of yours? What's-his-fuck? Roger Jones?

Roger Jones sells homes! Z yelled, raising her beer bottle to the sky.

Sly Girl laughed. We all laughed. Except Kayos.

How much are we gonna ask for in the ransom note? Kayos asked.

A cool million, I said.

She shook her head. That's too much. He doesn't have that.

Sure he does. Have you *seen* real estate prices in Vancouver?

He doesn't just have money like that lying around, Mercy.

Well, he'll have to get a loan then, I said.

Why don't we ask him for a reasonable amount? Something they can actually afford.

Kidnapping is not about making the ransom affordable, I said. It's about asking for what you want. And getting it. The alternative is not an option, so whatever the amount is, they'll pay it. They can re-mortgage the house if they have to.

Sounds like you've done this before, she mumbled.

Nope, I'm a kidnapping virgin! I raised my beer in a toast, and clinked it against everyone's bottle.

Not for long, said Z. She smiled at Mac. Mac put her arm around Z and pulled her close.

We need that money, Mac said, watching Kayos with careful eyes. For our new home. Once we get the cash, we can make a deposit on a condo right away, get the fuck out of here. We know they can afford it, Kayos. His ugly mug is on billboards all over the city, for fuck's sakes. We could probably ask for two mill and he'd pull it out of his ass.

But we're not greedy, Z said, grinning.

Outside, two people started screaming and swearing at each other, junkies fighting over money or drugs or both. I won't miss this place, I said. Not one little bit.

MAC

My neighbourhood is a ten-block hell, crawling with the rejects of society. Yeah, I wanna quit the DTES. Yeah, I wanna get the fuck out of Dodge. I've wanted to get out of here for as long as I've been alive. I want to live on a quiet street where people mow their lawns and barbeque on Saturdays, where they wash their cars, and where kids and dogs can run around and play and roll in the grass without getting pricked by a syringe. Is that too much to ask?

itz Mac'$ birfday. ima pull out all da $topz. got a few bottlza champayne, da reeel good $hit, not dat cheapa$$ $parklee wine, got her a DQ cake w/ happy 18 Mac we ♥ U!!!! on it. & ima $how her my new peece i put up ju$t 4 her. itz her, but az a pin-up grrl. $uper $exy. wearing HI heelz & a red je$$ica rabbit dre$$. blOwing a $moking pi$tol in her hand. O ya. i did it on da wall of da $ugar factoree cuz $he told me $he goez down dere 2 think $umtimes. ju$t $tare out @ da portz & B alone. plu$ $hez $o $weet $o da $ugar factoreez perfect 4 a portrait of her. hahaha. O, god, gimme my Mac. & when she dyez, take her & cut her out in little starz & she'll make da face of heavn so fyne dat all da wurld will B in love w/ nyte! O god, i love her 2 much. i'm talking capital L-O-V-E, man. seerius. we gonna have fun 2nite tho, boiii! gonna treet my grrl ryte! thingz R $o good w/ her. evn tho all dis $hitz goin down, lyke $ly got fucked up real bad den we got robbed & lo$t evrything, i know itz gonna be OK cuz we got each other. ya, sure, we got da re$t of da grrlz 2, but me & Mac got each other 4 lyfe, know what i'm $ayin? i'm down 4 that grrl 4 lyfe. 4 real. & i know $he feels da $ame 4 me.

SLY GIRL

Mac's birthday was fun. I got real fucked up. Drank a bottle of champagne and passed out on the couch. I dreamt I was smokin crack and shootin heroin in the kitchen, and Mac saw me but she didn't care. She just drank some orange juice out of the carton in the fridge like she always does and left me alone. Then I had some nightmares. Real bad ones. About things that happened to me before. Fucked-up things. When I woke up around four in the morning, I was soaked in sweat. I felt like shit and tried to forget all my dreams and all my memories and my whole entire life, but I felt so awful. I wanted a hit real bad right then. All the drugs we had got stoled, though, so there was nothin in the house. Everyone else was in bed. Thug was pawin at the door, so I took him out for a little walk. I thought if I happened to run into someone I knew who had some shit, maybe I'd score. But I didn't have any cash on me. It all got took when we got robbed.

Down? A guy asked me when I passed the Latino Corner.

I stopped walkin. Nodded slowly. I hadn't done heroin since before I went to detox, almost a year ago, but I'd thought about it. Every. Single. Day.

Thug let out a low growl as the guy put his hands in his pockets. Whatchu want girl?

H.

How much?

Just a ten bag, but ... I don't have any cash on me right now. Can you front me?

Fuck off, he snickered and waved his hand.

Please, man. I...

He looked me up and down, wrinkled up his nose. Then his eyes fell on Thug.

Thug looked up at him and growled again. I gave his leash a yank and he stopped.

Your dog. He patted Thug's head.

Yeaah.

I'll give you a ten bag for your dog.

I looked down at Thug and he looked up at me like he understood what was goin on, his amber eyes all shiny and scared. I looked at the guy. His bony yellow face was shadowed under the brim of his hat. He was no one I knew. I looked at Thug again and he whined.

I, uh, I...

I'll throw in a couple of Percocets, he said.

I watched Thug step back and forth around a puddle, his muscles ripplin beneath his coat. I thought about how Mac had said he was my responsibility. Thought about how I'd always wanted a dog. For as long as I could remember. And now that I finally had one, I was about to sell him for a hit of lousy Latino smack. I—I can't. Sorry.

Go on, get your fiending ass outta here then. He spat through his teeth, and a shiny wad landed on Thug's paw.

Me and Thug hurried away, and I ran him back to the house. I locked all the locks on the door and put the two chains across. I went to my room and curled up on my bed, buried my face in Thug's fur. I'm sorry, boy. I am so, so, sorry. And then the tears came. I cried hard and long and let Thug lick the tears from my cheeks. Finally, I slept without dreamin.

I turned eighteen today. In the eyes of the law, I am officially an adult. And I gotta say, for someone who came up like I did, I got things pretty good. As shitty as life has been for me, things are pretty good right now. Hell, I'm surprised I even made it to eighteen, the way my life has played out. But tonight I actually felt like I have a real family. My girls are good to me. They got me an ice cream cake and champagne and we smoked fat blunts sealed with honey oil. Once we all had a good buzz on, Z took us down to the sugar factory and showed us this painting she'd just finished.

I have to wonder what's going through that girl's head sometimes, man. She had painted me up there, ten feet high for the world to see. I mean, it wasn't exactly me, it was like a cartoon, Playboy Bunny me, but you could still tell. There was no fuckin way I wanted my portrait up there for public consumption. I didn't want to be recognized on the street as that girl from the sugar factory graffiti, you know? I didn't want the cops to recognize me from it. I was having none of it. I wanted to tell her to paint over it. Right fuckin now. I looked at all the girls, trying to gauge their reactions. Decide how I should handle this.

Mercy had her arms crossed over her chest and one eyebrow raised, probably expecting me to explode. Sly Girl just stared up at it in awe; head tilted back, jaw dropped, her droopy eye rolled back. Kayos had her lips pursed; she looked like maybe she wanted to see herself up there instead. But then when I saw the look in Z's eyes, so hopeful, so proud, just bursting with … with goodness and love, I knew I couldn't say anything. Except that it was amazing. Except, thank you.

We smoked a joint, then walked home, Z and me linking arms. She's changed me, that girl has.

Everyone proceeded to get shit-faced, and we made popcorn and played some old-school hip-hop tapes and danced around the living room with our clothes on backwards.

Later, in bed, snuggling under our blankets, Z asked me, So, my lady, how does it feel to be eighteen?

It's kind of strange, you know? Being stuck in this weird place between being a child and being an adult, and not really ever having been either.

MERCY

I had worked out all the logistics of the kidnapping, and on the weekend I stole a bunch of magazines. When I got home, Sly Girl and I worked on pasting together the ransom note:

FOR SAFE RETURN OF YOUR DAUGHTER LEAVE 1,000,000 IN CASH INSIDE A BLACK BACKPACK IN THE MAIN LIBRARY, 7TH FLOOR STUDY CUBICLE CLOSEST TO THE SHAKESPEARE SECTION. SATURDAY AT NOON. PUT A BOOK WITH A RED COVER ON TOP OF IT AND LEAVE. BOTH OF YOU COME. NO COPS! TELL NO ONE. OR ELSE THE GIRL GETS IT!

On Saturday, Sly Girl would be at the library, waiting and watching for the drop. Kayos would be at home in Shaugnessy, wringing her hands, waiting for her parents to return from the library. Mac, Z, and I would be in the house, taking care of the kid and waiting for Sly Girl's call. When it was safe, Sly Girl would pick up the backpack and go for a coffee at the Blenz in Library Square. I would meet her there, and drive her and the payload home. Later I'd steal a car and drop the kid off on the Jones' doorstep late at night—ring the bell and take off. No one would be hurt, and we'd be back on top of our finances. Then we could go condo shopping. Someone should congratulate me. It was the best and easiest money-making scheme I'd ever had.

KAYOS

Friday was a Pro-D day, so I didn't have school. In the afternoon, Mom was going to a bridal shower in Burnaby, and Roger would be at work. It was the perfect opportunity to get Laura out of the house. All morning I felt like shit. I couldn't eat, my stomach hurt, and a splintering headache chipped away at my brain.

What's wrong, sweetie? You don't seem yourself, Mom said.

Uh, cramps.

Oh, okay. Well, you take it easy today. Watch a movie or something. Take Laura to the park if you want, get some fresh air.

Yeah, sure.

Oh, and if you get a chance, can you throw a couple of loads of laundry in? Thanks, hon.

Mmhmm. I felt a plummeting elevator in my guts. Here I was, about to scam my own mother out of a million bucks. The least I could do was her laundry.

Did you want to come to the bridal shower? We could bring Laura.

No, no. That's okay. I tried to smile. You have fun though.

Alright. She smiled. Someday we'll be planning your bridal shower.

Mom!

She gazed at me, and her green eyes filmed over. You're growing up so fast. I'm so proud of you, Kayla.

I put my head down on the counter.

Do you have a boyfriend?

No.

So it's just girlfriends you spend all your time with?

Uh-huh.

Well, when do I get to meet them?

I don't know, Mom.

Do you want to have them over for a slumber party this weekend?

No.

Next weekend?

No!

Do you need some Midol, sweetie?

I lifted my head. Yeah.

She went to the bathroom and came back with two blue pills. She gave them to me with a glass of milk. Alright, I've gotta scoot. But have a good day, and I'll see you around four-thirty or five.

Okay. Bye. Have fun.

She gave me a kiss on the cheek and left. I watched out the window as her little red Beetle pulled away, and then I called Mercy. Yo, it's me. They're gone.

Be right there, she said, and hung up.

I saw my mother today.

MERCY

Alright, they're both gone. Let's go.

Mac lay on the couch, staring out the window. She sighed and reached for her cigarettes.

You're into this, right? You think this is a good idea?

Yeah. It's a really good idea. If it works.

Oh, it's going to work. I grinned. I grabbed the ransom note and the car keys. Okay, got everything?

Yeah.

Let's do this.

My heart drummed against my chest on the drive up to Shaughnessy. But what did I have to be nervous about? This was simple. I did dirt riskier than this every day and had no problems. What was wrong with me? Maybe because it was a new thing. Maybe because I knew it was our only shot at getting our money back. Maybe because I didn't really like kids. Maybe, in my heart of hearts, I was afraid that something would go wrong.

KAYOS

Okay, here's a bag with some cookies and juice and stuff in it. This one has some of her toys. I held out two plastic bags to Mac.

Wait, wait. Hold up. We can't take her toys, Kayos, Mercy said.

Why not? It'll be better if she can have some familiar things around.

Because it will be obvious that it was an inside job. Think about it. Mercy pried the bunny from Laura's hands, and she began to cry.

See? You won't want to listen to that for two days.

I'll get her some new toys, don't worry about it. We have to play this cool.

Laura started to scream and freak out. I grabbed the bunny and gave it back to her and she stopped. I wiped the snot from her face with a paper towel. Yo, at least let her have her bunny. One stuffy is believable.

Okay, fine. Whatever.

Just try not to freak her out, okay? She's … kind of shy.

She'll be fine. She's in good hands, Mac said, and hoisted Laura onto her hip. She handed her a cookie from the plate on the counter and Laura sucked on it, watching Mac with her huge blue eyes.

And you gotta feed her like every other hour, just a little bit. Half a banana, a couple cookies, a tiny sandwich or whatevs.

We'll feed her, Kayos.

But don't give her any candy or else she gets crazy.

Okay.

So, let's hear your story, Mercy said.

Okay. I put Laura down for a nap and fell asleep watching a movie on the couch. When I woke up and went to check on her, I found the note in her bed.

And then what do you do?

I call my mom.

Good.

I don't think we should have any contact until this thing is done, Mac said. Just in case they check your phone records or something.

What? How am I gonna know she's okay? What if something goes wrong?

Mercy shrugged. You'll just have to have faith in us I guess.

No. I shook my head. No way. Not for this. You need to text me. Just put it in code. Say the movie was really good, if everything's okay. Something like that.

They looked at each other.

And say the movie sucked, if shit hits the fan and I need to come down there.

Mac nodded. Okay, that'll work.

But everything is going to be totally fine, Mercy said. You don't need to worry about a thing.

She's right, Mac said. Okay, so here's the deal: on Saturday at noon, Sly Girl will be stationed at the downtown library. Me, Mercy, and Z will have Laura at home. As soon as Sly confirms that the cash is in the bag, we'll drop Laura off on the doorstep and ring the bell. You'll answer the door. Got that?

Yeah.

But you didn't see anybody drop her off. No car. Nothing.

I didn't see anything. She was just there on the doorstep.

Right.

She'll be home safe and sound in less than forty-eight hours, Mercy said as she checked her watch.

I started chewing my nails. Promise?

Relax, okay? This is so easy. You don't need to worry about anything.

What if they can't get the cash?

Mercy looked around the room.

She took in the vaulted ceilings, my mom's Swarovski crystal collection, the stained glass window over the sink, the marble countertops, the leather furniture.

They will, she said.

SLY GIRL

Mac and Mercy sent me out to sling after they brought Kayos's little sister home. It was rainin sideways. I didn't want to be out there. I wanted to stay home with all them and watch *Dora the Explorer* and look at picture books with Kayos's sister and eat cookies, but I knew that one of us had to be out there. It was welfare Wednesday and the streets would be hoppin. I took the G-pack and Thug out to our corner. Business was steady from the time I got out there. A couple of Johns pulled up lookin for a date. God, I hated that. Go piss up a rope. Just because I'm Native and standin on a corner in the Downtown Eastside doesn't make me a whore. There was a time I would've jumped into their cars for ten bucks or a line of baby-powdered coke, but now, the thought of doin all those gross sex things made me want to puke. I just shook my head and pointed them toward East Cordova and Gore, my old corner, and held on tight to Thug's leash.

My old friend Blue came by to cop. I hadn't seen him for a while, and he was lookin pretty rough. His lips were all purple and puffy, and he had nasty scabs on his face. Me and Blue used to hang out a lot when I was livin on the street. We'd cop together, get high together, look for ground-scores, look out for each other while the other one slept. He was just a little punk Indian kid from Manitoba. Blue worked the Fruit Loop in Stanley Park, sometimes Davie.

Hey, cousin.

Hey, Blue, how you doin? I laughed.

Aw, you know, strikes and gutters. He reached down to pet Thug. You got any Oxy today?

Nah, just rock.

Okay, um, can I get a half-ball?

Sure. So how you been anyways? I slipped him the chunk of crack wrapped in tinfoil as he slid the cash into my other hand.

Well, I got some bad news a couple days ago, actually. He stared at the dirty sidewalk beneath us. He tugged on one of the spikes lining his black hoodie, then jammed his hands in his pockets.

What?

I, um, I'm positive. He shrugged.

Oh.

Uh-huh.

Blue...

Yeah.

Aw, man, I'm sorry. That's so shitty, eh.

Yeah, kinda sucks. He looked up at me.

I stared into his soft, dark eyes. I thought of all the times we'd shared cigarettes, pipes, needles. I felt a wave surge through my stomach, and suddenly my legs felt like Jell-O. I put my hand on Thug's head to steady myself.

He looked away. So... yeah. Maybe you should think about getting tested.

I nodded.

I'm sorry, Rachel, he said, clenchin the rock in his fist.

Yeaah.

I gotta go.

I looked down at Thug and he whined and cocked his head to the side the way he does when he knows somethin's wrong. Then my next customer was pushin cash into my hand before I had a chance to think anymore on what Blue had said.

di$ kid iz pretty damn cute. $he lookz a lot lyke Kayos. same pale red hair, eyez lyke da sea. i think i'm good w/ kidz. dey don't cry & $ulk around me cuz i'm not hearin it. Laura—we nicknamed her Lil' Lo—was a bit whinee @ 1st, but now we got her $ettled in, $he $eemz happee E-nuff. Mercy got $um $tuffed animalz & gamez 4 her, we rented $um kidz muvees. evrybudeez Xcited. Mac iz makin food, Mercy iz dancing around & $inging about u$ being millionaire$, & Lil' Lo & me'$ on da couch watchin *Antz*. when $he Cs me eating my chocolate bar $he $tix out her lil hand & $ez: COOKIE! & $hez ju$t 2 cute so i break off a peece of my ree$e & give it 2 her. $he $huvs it all in her mouth & putz out her hand 4 another peece. $o i laff & give her da re$t of it.

  i think mebbe i'd lyke 2 have a kid 1 day. mebbe me & Mac cood have a kid 2gether. if Mac wuz in2 it, i mean. dat cood be cool.

What the fuck happened? What the fuck? Z!? What did you give her?

Z's eyes are huge and scared and we are both staring at Laura lying sideways on the couch with these red welts all over her face and puffed-up chipmunk cheeks. Her breathing sounds like Darth Vader, and her eyes won't focus.

I don't know … I don't know! We were sitting here watching the movie, and everything was fine! Then all of a sudden, she starts making these wheezing noises and her face swells up. I …

Then, both our eyes fall on the orange wrapper crumpled on the floor. Reese's Peanut Butter Cups. I pick it up.

Did you give these to her?

Just a half of one! A quarter of one! Oh, *shit*.

Jesus! Fuck!

Mercy skips into the room singing, *If I had a million dollars, if I had a million dollars, I'd buy you a fur coat, but not a real fur coat, that's cruel!* She looks at Laura, then looks at us, and then back at Laura. Oh. This isn't good, is it?

Text Kayos right now.

What should I say? She pulls out her phone.

911. Get down here now. I turn back to Laura. No, wait! Wait. Say, the movie sucked. Here, let's get her sitting up. I go to Laura and try to prop her up against the couch. She shrieks, her face turning purple, and slumps onto her side. I try to move her again.

Oh no, says Z, covering her ears. Don't do that.

I turn to her. Well, what the hell am I supposed to do? Huh? Tell me. I turn back to Laura. Shh, you're okay. Don't worry.

She stops screaming, but her breathing is plugged. She seems to be choking on her own tongue.

Get me some water.

Z runs to the kitchen, and Mercy picks up a doll on the floor and sits beside Laura on the couch. She makes the doll move in her hands and speaks in a funny squeaky voice. Hey there, little Missy! What's going on?

Laura's eyes roll from Mercy to the doll.

Oh yeah, I'm talking to you! You want to sit up and chill out or what?

Laura splutters, giggles, coughs.

Z returns with the water and gives it to me. Mercy manages to get Laura sitting up, and I tilt the glass of water into her mouth. She gasps and the water dribbles down her chin. Bubbles of spit ooze from her lips. I pull up her shirt to wipe it away and see red blotches all over her tummy and chest. Her breathing sounds like a broken radiator.

Is there something in her mouth?

Mercy shrugs. How the hell should I know?

Well, open it.

Open it?

Yeah.

You open it.

Fine. I hand her the glass of water and pry Laura's mouth open with two fingers. I feel around in her mouth and the back of her throat to see if something is blocking her airway.

It's clear. I get a flash memory of doing a mouth sweep once before, on my mom. Laura starts crying, but Mercy makes the doll dance and talk again, and Laura stops to stare at the doll. But her eyes are glazed and her lips are bluish and her little chest is puffing so hard to get each breath.

Should we ... should we call 911? Z asks.

Are you kidding? Mercy says. She's going to be fine! Look at her, she's laughing.

It's half true. She's smiling a little and drooling a lot. She reaches for the doll and Mercy pulls it away. She reaches again and Mercy lets her have it. She seems like she might be okay. Maybe. Mercy and I look at each other, and I see my own fear reflected back to me in her eyes.

Kayos bursts through the door then. What is it? What's wrong? She vaults over the couch and examines Laura. Oh my God. What happened?

She ate a peanut butter cup, but she's totally fine, Mercy says, leaning back into the couch, studying her new manicure.

She's not totally fucking *fine*, Mercy! Her lips are blue! Kayos sticks her ear beside Laura's mouth. She's not breathing!

She's breathing.

You fucking idiots. She scoops Laura up and heads for the door.

Whoa, whoa, whoa. Mercy leaps off the couch. What are you doing?

I'm taking her to the hospital. I've got a cab waiting outside.

I'm sorry, but you're not.

What?

Mercy stands between Kayos and the door. I think you're overreacting just a teensy bit here. Yeah, okay, we had a little scare, but she's looking a lot better now, so we can all just relax and stick to the plan. She's already doing *so* much better than five minutes ago. Right, Mac?

Probably. I move to stand near Kayos so I can get a better look at Laura. Her skin still has the welts, and sort of a blue tinge.

She needs to get checked by a doctor. It could get worse, Kayos whines.

If you walk out that door, we lose a million dollars.

She could *die!*

I can't let you leave, Mercy says, crossing her arms over her chest.

You're crazy! Kayos pushes past her but Mercy stands her ground in front of the door.

If you want to get past me, you're going to have to kill me, because I am not letting you fuck up this deal for us.

Hold on, Mercy, Kayos, I said.

In the time it takes to say I'm sorry, Kayos reaches into her waistband, pulls out her gun and shoots Mercy twice in the chest. I reach for my gat as she turns hers on me and pop her in the head before she can pull the trigger. She crumples to the floor, still holding onto Laura with one arm. Mercy slides to the ground in slow motion, leaving a streak of bright blood on the door behind her. I kneel beside her, squeeze her hand.

Mercy! Are you okay?

Yeah, just a scratch. A scratch. She laughs, and blood gurgles out her mouth.

Hang on, you'll be alright.

I'm sorry, Mac, she whispers. I fucked up.

It's okay, Merce. You're gonna be just fine.

How do you know?

Because bad bitches don't die.

She smiles up at me. Then a cloud passes over her eyes and she's gone.

Laura is crying and, I realize, so am I. I look over at Z on the couch, her face as white as the moon, her sad, scared eyes holding mine.

Did that just happen?

Yeah, she whispers.

I fold into the floor, holding my head in my hands. The smell of shit fills the room. I don't know if it's Laura, Mercy, Kayos, or all three.

Z comes to me and puts her arms around me. She smoothes my hair and kisses the top of my head. Together, we listen to the sirens wail down the block, getting louder and louder until they are upon us.

VANCOUVER

It is said that I am the youngest metropolis in North America, one of the youngest cities on Earth, but sometimes... sometimes, I feel so old.

SLY GIRL

When Thug and I got home, there were those yellow police banners on the door. Inside, the house looked like the set of a horror movie. There was blood everywhere. Hello? I called out. I was afraid that someone had come and murdered all my friends and now they were waitin to kill me. I didn't know what to do. I phoned Mac, Mercy, Kayos, and Z, but no one answered. I ran to my room and packed a bag of clothes and some food for Thug and left. I had about a thousand dollars in cash on me. I didn't know where to go, cuz no hotels will take dogs, and I couldn't just leave Thug there in the house with a serial killer probably hiding in the closet.

I wandered around Gastown for a while, tryin to figure out what to do. Got a two-dollar slice and a can of Coke. I decided I could just walk around until daylight and figure out what to do in the mornin. Maybe I'd hear from one of the Roses and know what the hell was goin on by then. But it started rainin, and I was dog-tired, my legs felt so heavy, and my feet were so sore. Stayin up all night wasn't as easy to do without meth or coke or K or somethin. Without really plannin it, I ended up at this old squat where I used to crash sometimes when I was homeless. I went in the side door and the usual suspects were there, sprawled around the floor, shootin up, snortin, and smokin drugs. In a way, it felt like comin home.

needle$$ 2 $ay, we nevr got our million. Kayos & Mercy were pronounced dead wen da paramedix arrived & Laura wuz givn a $hot of adrenaline & ru$hed 2 da ho$pital. Mac & i were takn down 2 da $tation 4 que$tioning, both R heart$ $hattered in a million little peeces. dey $plit u$ up in2 diffrnt interrogation roomz. i tryd my be$t 2 protect her, but i knew $he wuz fucked Bcuz $he wuz 18. $he did a bettr job of protecting me & cleared me of NE & all involvement in da kidnapping or da $hootingz. i wuz allowed 2 go live w/ my parentz again on da condition dat i go bak 2 skewl & B indoorz by 11pm evry damn nyte.

  it wuz hell. my lyfe turned in2 a living hell.

  after $kewl i wud ju$t wandr up & down granville $treet, waiting 2 die. i'd $tay out till 11 $o my parentz & sisterz wud B in bed wen i came in & not ha$$le me. i coodn't paint. i coodn't draw. i coodn't wryte. i coodn't eat, $leep, nothing. nothing cood make me bettr. dey locked up my love. i had nothing left.

Well, here I am in hell, a.k.a. Surrey Remand. I'm awaiting trial. It keeps getting pushed back. I don't even know what day it is now. I just go where I'm supposed to when they tell me to. I've been in here about three weeks. It's loud. Chicks are always screaming and throwing tantrums and shit. I guess a lot of them are detoxing in here. I try to keep my head down, not talk to anyone. They all want to know my story, find out what I can do for them, get for them. I don't tell them I'm the leader of the Black Roses. I don't tell them about my L.C. connections. When they push it, I say I got arrested for shoplifting.

My cellmate is Nikki. She's a meth addict. She has stringy blonde hair and acne, and her body looks like it's eating itself. She is eighteen and being tried as an adult, like me. She was arrested for robbing a convenience store. I try not to listen to her as she yammers on about her boyfriend, her ex, her parents, her pimp, her cravings, her kids, everything. But sometimes it's easier to listen to her than get caught up in the thoughts in my own head. I don't like to think about my trial, about what's gonna happen to me. My lawyer says we have to stay positive, but that's pretty fuckin hard to do when two of your best friends are dead and you're stuck in a five-by-eight cell with a meth head. My lawyer is kind of a douche. Hank got him for me. He's got yellowy bags around his eyes and he smells like vodka and car air freshener. We're gonna plead self-defence, because that's what it was. I don't know what will happen.

I miss Z. I know they let her off, and I'm glad. Why should

both of us have to suffer? I've tried calling her about a thousand times, but her cell phone's been disconnected and the line at her parents' just rings and rings. God! I really miss her. If only they'd just let me talk to her. I wish I could have visitors in here, but I'm not allowed any until after my trial. Except for Larry, my lawyer. He brings me smokes, chocolate bars, a book, once. *The Client.* Larry's alright, I guess. Hank says he's the best.

Sometimes, at night, after I hear Nikki snoring, I let myself go, and I cry. I cry and I cry and I cry. Wake up in the morning and my pillow's all damp, and I just wish I could go back in time and erase everything that happened after Mercy said she had this brilliant idea. I could've just shut her down then, told her it was a stupid plan and would never work. But I didn't. I went along with it. And I fucked up everything forever.

For the first time in my life, I'm scared. I'm really fuckin scared. And the worst part is, there's not a goddamn thing I can do about it.

ye$terday i $kipped $kewl 2 go 2 Mac's court d8. wen da judge read her $entence i felt my in$ydes bein ripped out.

Guilty.

my Mac wuz found guiltee of po$$e$$ion of a controlled $ubstance w/ intent 2 traffik, extortion, kidnapping, & 2nd-degree murder. $he wuz tryd az an adult & $entenced 2 lyfe w/out parole.

she iz da love of my lyfe & da onlee per$on who evr gave a $hit about me & now $he iz being takn away frum me. 4evr. i didn't realyze it until da ladee next 2 me put her hand on my $houlder, but i wuz wailing lyke a $tuck pig. da noyze came frum $umwhere deep in$yde my gutz. i coodn't $top it. i looked in2 dat ladee's ruined face & mo$$ green eyez & i knew who $he wuz. i knew dat once, $he had been beautiful, lyke her daughter wuz now. $he folded me in2 her & held me w/ her pipe-cleener armz & let me cry & $not all ovr her pink track-$uit. $he $hushed me & patted my bak, ju$t lyke a real mom wud. evn az i fell apart in her armz, i wanted 2 blame her $umhow. if $he had been a better mom & not a junkee crack whore, Mac nevr wud have gottn in2 di$ lyfe, $he nevr wud have ended up here, & we cood have been 2gethr 4evr & been $o $O happee.

now $he'z in a cage fo 25 fuckin yearz, & wat do i have 2 live 4? not a goddamn thing.

VANCOUVER

The streets are slick with rain and the girl walks alone, seeing only the concrete beneath her feet. Her head used to be full of colours, but she doesn't paint anymore. Instead, she makes etchings on her body with razor blades and waits to feel something, anything. Her heart sits raw and heavy inside her bird-like ribcage. Her eyes, dark as a storm cloud, were once sparkling with hope, excitement, passion. Now they are dull and downcast, and they hardly see the world around her. Like so many others in my city, she is ready to lay herself down in the street and give up.

I have watched her grow from infancy, watched her throw back her head and laugh into the rain. I watched her fall in love—with art, with the world, with life. I know she could have done anything, she could have been anything, but not now. Not ever.

She walks and walks until she finds her sister-friend, the laughing one with the sleepy eye. From her, she buys powder the colour of sand. It is enough. She also borrows tools: a needle, spoon, and tourniquet. She hugs her friend goodbye, knowing it is the last time she will see her.

As she lies down in the tall grass, the clouds expand around her, the sky opaque and shimmering, like a pearl.

MAC

After my trial, a cruiser took me out to Maple Ridge, and I was admitted to Alouette Women's Correctional Facility. They took me into a cold little white room with a doctor's bed-table thing. They made me strip. Then, this ugly-ass female guard with poodle hair snapped on a pair of gloves.

This is gonna suck for me, isn't it? I said.

Lie down, please, she said, and proceeded to stick her hand up my cunt and feel around for awhile.

Jesus.

Turn over please.

Oh, God.

Turn over.

I don't want to.

The other guard put her hands on my shoulders and flipped me over in one swift movement. Then the poodle lady spread my ass cheeks and felt around up there for awhile.

Ow! Fuck!

If you clench, it hurts more. Just try to relax.

I ground my teeth together and tried to think of something else. Swimming. Birds. Convertible rides on sunny days. *Ow!*

Okay, you can get dressed. She sounded disappointed that she didn't find a gram of cocaine and a pack of razor blades up my ass. She handed me my prison uniform.

Purple, my favourite.

Poodle-lady raised an eyebrow. The two of them stood

near the door, watching while I dressed. I wanted to crawl under a floor tile and stay there.

They escorted me back out into the main hall where I was given two tiny bars of soap, a black plastic comb, a white toothbrush, a tube of Crest, a small plastic bottle of bleach, two latex gloves, and printed instructions on how to make a dental dam. I snickered, and the guard looked at me as if I had murdered her first-born.

Let's go. She took my arm and led me down the hall.

I kept my eyes down so I didn't have to look at anyone. They hooted and whistled at me from their cells as we walked down the dark corridor.

Home sweet home, the guard said as she flicked a switch. There was a metallic buzz, and the door slid open.

I stepped inside. Another buzz and the electric door closed behind me.

Hands.

I stuck my hands through the steel bars and she uncuffed me. She pocketed the cuffs and walked away.

I looked at my cell. It was a concrete room with a single bed in one corner, a steel toilet and sink in the other. There was no seat on the toilet. There was no window. A grey army blanket, pale blue sheets, and a pillowcase lay folded on the end of the bed. As I stood staring at the stained, brown mattress, I felt lonelier than I ever had in my life.

I sat down on the bed. My body felt like it was made of concrete. I closed my eyes and listened to the noises of maximum security. Someone was singing, someone was hollering for the guard, someone was talking, someone was laughing, someone was praying.

I made the bed, fluffed up my paper-thin pillow, and lay down. I stared at the grey blanket with ALOUETTE stamped across it and thought about my dad. It was kind of funny, because this was the closest we had been in ten years, him being just down the road at Fraser Regional, but neither of us could visit the other because we were both locked up. Then I realized that he would get out before I did. Hell, maybe he would even come visit me.

Yo, new kid on the block! someone yelled.

Hey, new chick! What's your name?

There were whispers and shouts of excitement up and down the row.

Hey, girlee! We're talkin to you!

I rolled over and put the pillow over my head. I imagined I was back at home, cuddling with Z. I imagined her arms around me, telling me everything was gonna be alright. That everything would be alright, forever and ever and ever.

SLY GIRL

I felt pretty guilty about not goin to visit Mac yet. But Maple Ridge is just so far away, and I've been real busy tryin to get set up down here again. I'm tryin to find a place to live and someone decent to work for and all that. But when I heard about Z, I knew I had to go see Mac, tell her in person. Besides, I was the only one left to tell her.

Z had been strange the last time I seen her. I never knew she was into heroin, but I sold her what she asked for, a hundy bag, and told her how to cook it up.

Just take a teensy, tiny little bit, okay? I said. If you do all of this at once, it'll kill ya.

Okay. Perfect. Thanks, Sly. Oh, here, take this. She shoved a bank card into my hand. Savings. *6969.*

What's this for?

Just in case. Then she gave me a hug and told me she loved me and ran off down the alley.

If I had known, I never would've given it to her, I swear to God, I wouldn't have. But how could I have known? She told me she was bored. Said she needed a new hobby. Next day, she's found dead underneath her painting at the sugar factory, the needle still stickin out of her arm.

Soon as I heard, I went to the Carnegie. They let me call Mac's jail, helped me get the number and everythin, so I could find out the visiting hours. Today I left Thug with my friend Blue and hopped on the bus to Maple Ridge.

Just now I'm tryin to figure out the words to tell her. Just how the hell are you sposed to tell someone that the person they love the most in the world is dead? This might be the hardest thing I've ever had to do.

Soon as I saw Sly Girl walk in, I knew something was wrong. I felt it in the hollow of my stomach, like a rotten fruit. She scraped the chair back from the table and sat down as if she weighed a thousand pounds. Hi.

What's wrong?

Um, Z...

What?

She's gone.

Gone where?

She OD'd last night. I'm so sorry, Mac.

The room fell away and I couldn't see. I turned away from Sly Girl and coughed and gagged a little bit and thought I might puke. I tried to make myself breathe. I faced Sly Girl again, and she was cringing, tears leaked out of her destroyed eye. OD'd on what?

H, she whispered.

Z doesn't do heroin. There must be a mistake. It was someone else who just looked like her. Hope fluttered inside my chest. My lady wouldn't touch that shit. I knew it had to be a mistake.

Sly Girl swallowed. It was her.

Do you know who sold it to her?

She nodded, gazed at her ragged fingernails.

Who?

Me.

Fuck, Sly Girl! *Why?* My heart crumbled inside my chest.

Was it rat poison? A hot shot? What?

No! It was fine! It was good! She just did too much is all. I told her, Mac, I swear I did. I said just do a tiny little bit, a fingernail amount. I told her if she did the whole bag she would die.

I stared at Sly Girl, waiting for her to burst out laughing, to tell me this was a sick joke, that I was on *Candid Camera* or some shit, but she could hardly look at me and sat fidgeting in her chair. She was back full time on the pipe, that was obvious. I wished she was lying to me, but I knew she wasn't.

I'm so sorry, Mac. I wish I could've stopped her. I just...I didn't know, you know? I thought she just wanted to try it.

I took a deep breath. It's okay. It's not your fault.

She bit her bottom lip. Thank you, she whispered.

I held my head in my hands while my heart crumbled inside my chest. I had done this. I had done all of this damage.

I miss you, Mac. Everybody misses you.

I nodded. Now I knew she was lying. I closed my eyes and saw the quick and brutal flashes of how my night would unfold. The torn blue bed sheet. The improvised noose. First came the waves of doubt and then the final resolve. I had lost my love. I had nothing left worth sticking around for. And after twenty-five years on the inside, there would be nothing left for me to go back to.

I should get goin...I gotta work, Sly Girl said, snapping me out of my trance. I just wanted to let you know...I wanted you to hear it from me.

Yeah. Thanks.

I'll come visit you again soon though, she said, picking at her face.

Sure.

I promise.

I wanted to hug her or squeeze her hand or something, but there was no physical contact allowed. I wanted to tell her something to remember me by, to remember the Black Roses and all we had done and all that we were, but all I could think of to say was goodbye. And be good.

She bit her lip. You too. She looked for the guards out of the corner of her eye, then whispered, Black Roses forever.

Forever.

She stood up, and so did I. Be careful out there, Sly. The world is not your friend.

She nodded. Then a guard came and led me away.

SLY GIRL

For a short time, I had a family. For a short time, I had a place to call home. And I knew what it was to be loved. Now I can look back at that time in my life and say I was happy then, yeaah, I really was.

But now, my family has all gone to the Creator. And my home once again is the streets of the Downtown Eastside. But do you think these streets love you? These streets don't give a fuck about you. You could walk these streets for a million days and a million nights, and they wouldn't even know your name. These streets don't love anybody.

I got my dog still. I'm hangin in there. I do what the Black Roses taught me: walk softly, carry a big gun, hold my head up high.

EPILOGUE

SLY GIRL

I forgot about it for a while—guess it got lost inside some pocket—but a couple weeks after Mac strung herself up, I found Z's bank card and checked her savings account. There was $3,723.98 in there. I guess it was all the money she had saved from babysittin, birthdays, Christmas, whatevers. There it was. No one else was gonna do much with it, I figured, so I went to the teller and withdrew it all.

I think Z would've wanted me to have it. She was always generous like that. Givin out smokes, cookies—whatevers she had, she would give you without thinkin twice about it. She didn't care. She just wanted everyone around her to be happy. And you know, for the most part, we were.

Anyways, it was enough money for me to put down first and last on my own little room at the Stella Hotel. I had to pay an extra $500 for Thug to be able to stay, but I don't mind. He's worth it. Can you believe it? I have my very own room. It even has a hot plate and a mini-fridge! I make soup and ravioli and spaghetti from a can. Sure do miss Z's cookin somethin fierce, but I get by, I'm gettin by. Some days are harder than others. Some days I miss them all so much, and my heart hurts so much just to think on them that I don't even want to be in the world no more. Sometimes I get so sad and tired that I want to lie down in the middle of a busy intersection until I'm crushed right down into the blackness and disappear completely. But then I'll look at my dog and he'll kinda smile at me, and I know I won't ever leave him. I can't. I know my girls wouldn't want me to either. So I just keep goin. Keep on keepin on, like the song says. Yeaah. It's okay.

The carpet in my room is dusty-rose, it's stained and burnt and ass-dirty, but I don't care—it's *my* carpet. God, I wish the girls could see my room. Mercy would probably get some art and pretty fabrics and stuff to help me decorate, make it all sparkly and beautiful, but she's not around to help me, so it just stays the way it is for now. Maybe I'll buy one of the paintings that crippled guy on the corner does. He's pretty good, actually. Mac would've liked his stuff. She was into art. All kinds. She told me once when we were drunk that she had always wanted to study art history. That she was thinkin to maybe apply to UBC once we got our condo sorted out. That girl, she could've done anythin, eh. She could've been anythin. But then, somehow, so many things went wrong so fast. And I didn't know how to make them right again. Now they never will be. They never, never will be.

But when I think on Mac now, I like to think she'd be proud of me. For gettin straight, gettin my own place, meetin new people, all that.

The other people who live at the Stella Hotel are mostly junkies. But everyone's pretty nice. They all say hey to me and Thug when we go by in the hallway. My next-door neighbour is a crackhead named Henry who likes to do science experiments. He's always askin me to come over and check out his latest results. He showed me how to make a volcano with vinegar and baking soda and red food dye. Henry's real nice. Like when there's a line-up for our bathroom—cuz everyone on our floor shares the same bathroom—and he's in front of me, he always lets me go ahead of him. Once, when I saw a cockroach in my room, I started screamin cuz it was so big and ugly, and Henry came right over and banged on my door and asked me, What the hell's the matter? So I told him and he said, Is that all? I thought you were dying in here. And then he scooped the roach up with an empty Zoodle-O's can and chucked the whole thing out the window. Henry says not to worry even a little bit about them roaches because even the cleanest, richest, tidiest mansions get cockroaches sometimes, and you can't do nothin to stop them. They can even survive nuclear war, he says.

Henry shares his smokes with me sometimes, if I'm runnin low. And I'll give him a couple of mine if he's out. I guess that means we're friends. But if I don't feel like talkin to anybody, I can lock my door and put the chain across and no one can come in. If I don't feel like leavin my room all day, I don't have to. I can just hang out in my pyjamas, drink tea, and look at magazines. Just like we would sometimes do at the gang house if it was a real piss-pouring day. I always wish Kayos was around to make Jiffy Pop and watch a movie with me on those nasty days. She'd crank the music and demo her new ninja moves for us, eh. God, I'd give anythin to see one of her tornado spinnin kicks right now. Ha ha.

The heater in my room is real old, probably from the 1900s, but it works, and it gets real nice and toasty-warm in my room when it's all cold and rainy outside. Thug likes to curl up beside the heater and just sleep for hours. It's his favourite spot.

My favourite part of my room is the balcony. Well, it's not

really a balcony, it's just the landing on the fire escape, and I have to crawl out my window to get onto it, but I use it like a balcony and go out there and sit on it and have smokes and whatevers. I like goin out there at night and just watchin all the lights of the city. And sometimes, when it's not too cloudy, I can see the stars; they're far away and they're faint, but they're there.

I even have a job. A real, legit job. The fat white worker lady at the Carnegie helped me get set up with this Aboriginal Youth Entrepreneurship Program. I had to go to a bunch of meetings with an employment counsellor so we could figure out what I should do. Not just what I *can* do or what I'm good at, but what I *actually* want to do. I love animals, all animals, but dogs especially. So now I'm a professional dog walker. My company, ha ha, that sounds funny but it's true, it's called Luckydog Dog Walking. I guess I'm the CEO, ha ha. I even printed up these little business cards on the computer at the Employment Centre, and the counsellor chick helped me design these cute posters that I stick up on bulletin boards around the rich neighbourhoods. You wouldn't believe how many people have dogs but don't have time to walk them. My phone is always ringin. Most of my clients are in Yaletown, some are in the West End, and a few are in Shaughnessy. Shaughnessy is actually where I like to be walkin dogs the most cuz then I can keep an eye on Kayos's little sister, Laura. On Tuesdays and Thursdays I'm always in Shaughnessy to walk this beautiful Irish Setter named Sedona. She's a real gorgeous dog, all friendly and lovin. Sedona's house is just a few blocks away from Kayos's, so I make sure we always go past it at least twice. Sometimes Laura is out in the yard, playin with her dolls or drawin on the sidewalk with coloured chalk, kickin a soccer ball around with her mom or dad or whatevers. She's gettin real big now. She looks good. Healthy. Her hair is gettin long. It's bright red like Kayos's was. Spittin image.

The other day, Laura ran up to me all bouncin around with her bubble-wand. She wanted to pet the dog, eh. But her dad caught her by the arm and told her not to ever touch strange dogs without askin their owner if it's okay first. So then she looks up at me with all this watery hope in her eyes and says in her little kid voice, Can I pet your dog? Please?

Sure, I said. Go ahead.

Is she nice?

Yeah, she is. She's really nice.

Okay, she said, and reached out her hand.

And the crazy thing is, Laura will never know who I am, she'll never know about the Black Roses, all we did together, how much we loved her sister, but I will always, always look out for her. Forever.

ACKNOWLEDGMENTS

THANK YOU: Ben Parker, my first reader and secret weapon; David Chariandy for encouragement and kindness; Dennis E. Bolen for enthusiasm and moral support; Cathleen With for inspiration and conversation; Michael Christie for paving the way and lending me Henry; Gabe Schoenberg and Graffiti Tours New York for the tour and coco helado; Timothy Taylor for "graffiti as gifts"; Michael Chettleburgh for *Young Thugs*, which spawned the idea for this novel; Mark Kingwell for *Concrete Reveries: Consciousness and the City*; Odd Squad Productions Society; Misha Kleider, Alex Kleider, and Corey Ogilvie for *Streets of Plenty*; Chris Haddock for *Intelligence* (I'm still waiting for Season 3); Paul Schrader; William Monahan; Oliver Stone; Geoff (Tippi) Tomlin-Hood for locals only info, driving me around Strathcona, and always making time to hang when I'm in Vancouver; John Harkin for Vancouver info; Ron Little for car-starting info; everyone who shared their experiences of the street with me; the OGs; my agent, Hilary McMahon; the crew at Arsenal Pulp: Gerilee McBride for the book's design; Susan Safyan for making the editing process painless; Cynara Geissler; Brian Lam; to my family, thanks for being in my corner, especially my parents, John and Jennifer Little; and thank you, Warren, for food, shelter, and TLC, but thanks especially, for being down for life.

GLOSSARY

9: 9 mm gun

24's: 24 inch rims (on cars)

Alouette: Alouette Correctional Centre for Women, a
women's maximum security prison

bill: $100 dollar bill

blunt: a cigar that has been emptied of tobacco and filled with
marijuana

burners: disposable cell phones

connect: supplier of drugs

cooking: making crack

cop: pick up/buy drugs

deets: details

down: heroin

fiend: a person who craves a drug, e.g., crackfiend; fiending:
craving

G: gangster

G-pack: a street-ready package of drugs worth $1,000

gat: gun

ghost car: undercover police car, usually a sedan, easily
identified by the lack of hubcaps and a large antennae on
the roof

ground-scores: things of value found on the ground; ends of
cigarettes, change, lighters, etc.

H: heroin

Hastings shuffle: an erratic style of walking commonly seen in
pedestrians on East Hastings Street, often includes arm

flailing, pocket checking, and scratching of the skin, generally brought on by a drug-induced psychosis

hella: to describe a lot of something; similar to "very" or "really"

hotshot: such high purity heroin that a "regular dose" is lethal

hundy: $100

juvie: Juvenile Detention Centre

K: short form for thousand; or Ketamine, a psychoactive drug

key: kilogram

kiff: Second-hand items (usually stolen) that street people sell to make money; watches, jewellery, DVDs, frozen meat, etc.

L.C.: Lucifer's Choice Motorcycle Gang, a (fictional) highly organized and very violent international crime syndicate dealing mainly in narcotics, weapons, human trafficking, racketeering, and illegal gambling operations.

low pro: low profile, undetected

OG: Original Gangster; term of respect for long standing gang member

OPP: Other People's Property; a reference to Naughty by Nature's rap song

Oxy / Oxycontin: a semi-synthetic opiod analgesic prescribed to patients with chronic pain, when crushed up and snorted / injected for street use, it produces a quick and powerful high similar to heroin

PCP: Punjabi Canadian Princess

PoCo: Port Coquitlam, home of pig farmer / serial killer Robert Pickton

rags: bandanas; often seen worn by gangsters portrayed in the
   media

re-up: reload supply of drugs for street sales

rig: a needle or syringe used to inject drugs

rock: crack cocaine

Slurrey: derogatory name for Surrey, BC, a suburb of
   Vancouver notorious for gang violence

sick: awesome, cool, amazing

SRO: Single Room Occupancy apartment

U.P.: Unified Peoples, a (fictional) powerful street gang

Vancouver Special: a term used to characterize a particular
   style of common, cheap, box-like houses built in Vancouver
   from 1965–1985

ASHLEY LITTLE

studied creative writing at the University of Victoria (BC). Her debut novel, *Prick: Confessions of a Tattoo Artist* (Tightrope Books) was shortlisted for the ReLit Award and has been optioned for a film, for which she is writing the screenplay. She is also the author of the young-adult novel *The New Normal* (Orca Book Publishers). Ashley lives in the Okanagan Valley.

ashleylittle.com